The Testament

Of

I0533421

James Harper

ISBN-13: 978-1-962923-01-9

Cover design by: A. Dennison

Library of Congress Control Number: 2018675309

Printed in the United States of America

Dedicated to my brother, without whose encouragement, critiques, and many re-reads, this work would not exist.

Contents

Chapter One

I was sitting on the bridge of a ship that had actively tried to kill me a week ago, on my way to a job that would probably do the same. Inside and out was the absolute, impenetrable darkness of subspace. Photons don't stay in subspace. I don't know why, but somebody with a degree and too many collectible figurines probably does. Maybe they just don't like the place. Ask me, they got good taste. You can't really get it if you haven't been awake for a trip, and even most people who spend their lives in space never have. There are weird noises that sound like micrometeors hitting the hull, if you don't know that normal matter isn't endemic to subspace.

You feel heavy, or maybe like you're trying to move through mud. The ship creaks like it's going through nine different gravity wells at once, and you always feel like you should keep your back to a wall and both eyes open, though neither of those would do you an ounce of good if something went wrong in subspace. Paying attention to your ship will though, so when I heard the Braille pad clicking, I ran my fingers across it without delay. *Erebus* wasn't actively in a full dive into deep subspace, which was a marked improvement over the last time I went through this particular neighborhood of the universe, but we were getting close to the exit hack.

In my experience, this is when your ship usually tries to kill you if it's inclined that way. Erebus was never a benevolent god, so I took manual control. Most people don't ever actually touch the sticks unless they're pulling into a slip on the station. Piloting by hand through subspace and wild space, on the very same day no less, is usually described by most experienced pilots with words and phrases like "suicidal", "insane", and, in one notable instance, "The most out-of-fucking-sight dipshittery (sic) since the Omega War". But then most people don't have to purge their AI's as a routine measure to preserve their own lives. Imagine. Going for an entire career with the exact same AI on your ship the whole damn time. Crazy. As the Braille pad clicked down through the exit hack countdown, I closed my eyes. It didn't make a difference at the moment, but it would on the way out.

My left hand was on the pad, and my right was on the sub-drive throttle. Click. Three. Click. Two. Click. One. As soon as I felt the pins start to shift under the fingers of my left hand, I yanked the handle all the way back. I felt the always disconcerting feeling of pressure rushing away from my body, as though I were falling out of water and into the sky. Through the strange blur of sensation, I snatched the stick with my right hand. As soon as I felt it, I snapped my eyes open. The lights were still on their lowest setting, so I wasn't flash blinded when the photons started hitting my retinas again. I had a breath of thinking I was in the clear before the collision alarm started blaring that there was an object dead ahead and the pins shot into place underneath my left hand.

I pulled the stick back and even in the *Erebus*, I felt the g's sinking me into my seat. I clenched the muscles in my legs and abdomen, then I felt the mother of all speed bumps kick my old girl right in the belly. There was a screech like a harpooned whale from the beams of the ship, and then with a final scream of tortured metal it ripped off the lower engine. The constant rattle against the hull of micro debris shook *Erebus*. I cut speed and fell forward into my harness, then doubled the gain on the scanner. Shit. Everywhere. There were unidentified objects everywhere. I swerved around another one, then used my left hand to slam an ancient knife switch closed. As soon as the red light blinked off and the blue one blinked on, I spoke:

"Judas. Get me—" I cut off to swerve around another asteroid as it filled the viewscreen—"Get me a path out of this asteroid field, now." There was a half second delay, during which the panel of lights to the left side of the knife switch flickered like a firework, then a cool male voice replied:

"Very well, James. Pitch up, thirty-seven degrees... Mark. Yaw port, sixty-three degrees... Mark. Roll starboard, seventeen degrees, Mark." Another screech along the hull, sans tearing this time. "Judas..."

"Some damage is inevitable, James. Yaw right, forty-two degrees... Mark. Accelerate by three point five. Clear of debris field in three... two... clear."

I killed my speed and rolled *Erebus* so I could look at that field. I had a hunch. The field slowly rolled into view, vaguely silhouetted by the multitude of suns in the distance. I exhaled slowly.

"Damn."

"James..."

"I know. Those aren't asteroids... It's what's left of the *Alea*."

Chapter Two

The *Alea* went dark halfway through a voyage. No response on the q-graph, no arrival, no distress call sent, no calls from the q-graphs on the lifeboats. Two weeks later, a slight subspace ripple along its route indicated it may have just exited a jump, then nothing more. On the job order, this kind of incident is listed as

Failure To Arrive: Irregular Circumstance.

That was a bland way of saying it was a very weird case, which was exactly what had caught my eye about it. Weird cases were exactly why I did the job. Those were the cases that had a chance of giving me some answers.

Most of my jobs entail going out to investigate ships lost in wild space, adrift between the islands of the habitable systems, and find out what went wrong. Usually, the people who hire me are insurance agents looking for any excuse not to pay out for a ship that cost more than a space station, or the owners of ships trying to find any reason to get the insurance guy to pay out for a ship that costs more than a space station. There were other contracts certainly—sometimes people lost a ship that they didn't want enemies to find, and they would hire me to find it and either guide their forces to it, recover the ship, or, if necessary, scuttle it.

These were often more lucrative and more dangerous. They were also often of questionable legality and generally meant pissing off some faction or other in the end. I tended to stick closer to the find-and-investigate jobs.

Sometimes, you get a system full of caring types who will shell out my rate so that their citizens can find closure, and hey, reelect the prime minister or president or whatever body paid my fee. Occasionally jobs like this are dangerous, but that's not why people don't like doing them. Or at least it's not the whole story. People do dangerous shit all the time without even thinking twice. It's because this job is dangerous, and if you die, your corpse spends the next three hundred and fifty million years trying to find a nice star to warm up around, and that gets to them. Personally I don't really see the difference. Dead is dead, if my body wants to take the scenic route around the galaxy after I'm done with it, it's probably earned it.

The debris field was huge. I glanced at the schematics the Hwong-Howell Corporation had given me when I took the job. The *Alea* was generally shaped like a column, hexagonal in cross-section, with a forty-five degree bow and a few engine pods at the back. Reactors were all from Greyfeld General Fusion, like pretty much every other hauler made in the last hundred years. My eyes drifted to the row of numbers next to the vector diagram rotating on the screen. The Intersystem Registry of Cosmonautical Vessels had the *Alea* listed as being eight kilometers long, and it looked like at least half of that was drifting in the solar wind. Or would be, if there was a star within seventy light-years. I was scanning the debris field for anything big enough to warrant a spacewalk, or putting out a beacon, and Judas was trying to plot the likely trajectory of the main fuselage. The lights of Judas' monitor panel flickered, and I tilted my head in that direction. I kept my eyes on that field, though.

"James?"

I grunted in what could only be construed as an assenting manner by a devout optimist.

"Why do you disconnect me from my systems during subspace jumps?" Evidently Judas was a man of the faith. Irony strikes again.

"Because I don't trust you not to try a deep dive and kill me in a parallel dimension."

"How many times has that happened? Before, I mean. To you." No sarcasm there. I liked this Judas. That was a shame, really. I thought about it for a second.

"The number is non-zero."

"...Non-zero?" He asked dubiously.

"Decisively," I replied.

"...I see."

We lapsed into a long silence after that, Judas calculating our current position based on our exit point and changes in trajectory since, and me absently scanning the field, chin on my

7

hand and finger tapping my cheek. If I could have gone without an AI entirely, I would have. Unfortunately, humans just can't hack the math needed to plot a subspace course. Entering and leaving aren't hard: you just engage or disengage the drive slip in or out. Getting the course right is another matter entirely. I couldn't even afford to leave Judas off too long on a job. I needed him to do exactly what he was doing: keep track of our course changes so he would know roughly where we were. That was important for plotting a return course. Unless I was willing to take the long way home, which I was not, that meant I was stuck with the computer. Judas began to speak just as I saw something, and I missed it. I strained my eyes, looking for the anomaly in the wreckage. Where had it been?

There. A small glimmer of light, small enough that you might mistake it for the twinkling of the stars in the background if you weren't paying attention.

"Have you found something, James?" Judas sounded politely curious, like someone who was asking if you were ok when you had a coughing fit because you took a drink of water wrong.

"Maybe. I'm going in for a closer look."

I kept my eyes on the floating piece of debris as it seemed to slowly drift closer. Technically *we* were moving towards *it*, but that far out in space there's no real reference point, so it often looks like everything is always rushing at you instead of the other way around. I brought us to a relative stop with the twisted hunk of metal so close it could almost put an eye out, and I waited as it slowly tumbled end over end gracelessly. I tapped a rhythm on the handle of Judas' knife switch, impatient. Nothing on the first side, nothing on the second...

As the third side rolled through the viewport with nothing visible, I started to wonder if I was projecting, seeing what I expected instead of what was there. Judas piped up, curious again:

"James, what are we looking—"

He cut off as I slammed the knife switch open and cut his access to all systems, isolating his core unit from every other piece of equipment on the ship. My eyes were riveted on the piece of debris. More accurately, they were riveted on what was on the scrap: lines melted into the metal, still apparently glowing hot. Eerie curves and sinuous lines scrawled over jagged angles, every element of it somehow clashing horribly with every other part until the whole thing made me feel nauseous. It made my eyes hurt, like looking at the sun too long, but whereas the sun burned you with clean, pure light, this character made me feel like someone had splashed sewer water in my eyes. I had to look away almost immediately.

My stomach churned with a mix of anticipation and nerves. On the one hand, this was a lead on a trail I had almost begun to think was cold. On the other... Well. It wasn't a particularly pleasant trail to follow.

Without taking my eyes off it, I grabbed my satchel off the bulkhead. A case positioned to be easily accessible if, for some reason, you needed to access it without taking your eyes off the viewscreen. I flipped the latches on the battered leather and pulled out what most people these days think of as an archaic relic: a camera. A camera from pre-war days, much older even than that. I'd had to restore it after centuries of moldering in a museum, but it was a worthwhile expense for something that ran on gears and chemicals and therefore physically couldn't be hacked--or corrupted. I raised the viewing window to my eye and made sure the glyph was perfectly in focus and entirely in frame. I clicked the button, and the shutter actuated with that satisfying click you only get from old, inefficient Terra tech.

A small piece of paper popped out of a slot at the bottom, and I shook it for a moment while the image developed. Got it. The shot was good. They never match the crystal clarity of a modern image, but I didn't need that level of clarity either. I pulled a small steel case from the satchel, perfectly sized to hold exactly one picture, and slid the image inside quickly. The case snapped shut with a snick and I stowed it in the satchel for the moment. Then I fired the engines and made some space to think.

Chapter Three

As soon as I'd gotten *Erebus* on a parallel course a safe distance away from the debris field, I spooled down the engines to drift on inertia and took off Judas' blindfold. Then I grabbed the satchel and clambered down the ladder into the crew compartment of *Erebus*. I didn't bother to keep much onboard the ship; some weights and an aerobic rig, to exercise. A lot of old books, and some of my old art tools. I hadn't had much enthusiasm for hobbies outside of exercise in a while. I passed the small gym, the galley, and the med bay with its combined autosurgeon and hibernation pod. All necessities for someone who doesn't like to visit civilization much. Then descended another ladder to the single passageway on the lowest deck of the ship.

At the far end of the passageway was a door that looked like it belonged on a bank more than on a ship. Probably because it did. It was more than a century old, nearly impenetrable, and most importantly it used no electronics. Nothing even remotely resembling Von Neumann architecture. Good old-fashioned nano-machining all the way through. It was a find from a salvage job a few years back, and because of it I thought of the compartment behind it as *the vault*. I made my way down the corridor and entered a thirty-two-character alphanumeric password to correctly align the lock. There was a pause as some of the last mechanical components slipped into place, and then the hatch gave forth a weighty *chunk.* I threw the lever and entered the vault.

The vault is a compartment unlike most on my ship or others. I'd had the bulkheads reinforced more than most precious cargo hauler vaults were. I removed absolutely every kind of complex electronic device that had once been incorporated into the components. It was on a separate, chemical-based life support system, and the entire room was positioned, and rigged, so that I could manually blow it away from the rest of the ship if, or as I saw it when, the need arose. It would function as a life boat and had the necessary boosters and shielding to survive atmospheric reentry on most planets. The majority of the floor space was devoted to emergency rations, water, and the oxygen-and food producing plants that were the backbone of the chemical life support system. The starboard bulkhead held my modest armory. The port held a CC suit in its docking station, along with supplies for the suit and a maintenance kit. The rear was dominated by a large steel workbench and an old filing cabinet. The bench held various artifacts recovered from promising cases, most in some state of disassembly. The vault was an armory, supply cache, insurance policy, and evidence locker all rolled into one. I've been called paranoid more than once in the past. I always said that it's only paranoia if they're *not* out to get you.

I surveyed the vault briefly, making sure everything was as I had left it. Satisfied for the moment, I crossed the room to place the photo case on the work bench. I carefully moved the photo to a clip on the bulkhead. The grow lights in the vault mimicked sunlight almost perfectly, which suited my purpose just fine. I pulled two folders from the filing cabinet, removed the contents, and clipped them up next to the photo I had just taken.

The first, and oldest, was a blurry printout of a digital image. The original image had showed a small passenger ship drifting in front of a cerulean moon, clearly damaged and without power. My printout had been blown up to the point that it was mostly a pixilated mess, but if you looked hard enough you could make out a blurry collection of yellow-orange lines wrapping around the keel of the ship. Only a few were visible, but I knew they wrapped around the belly of the vessel and formed a bizarre symbol. It was the last image relayed from the emergency aid crew who responded to an SOS from the vessel in the picture, the OPV *Dawn Runner*. Six hours later the rescue vessel had rammed the *Dawn Runner* and they had both slammed into the moon below hard enough to make a new crater.

The second image was another photograph, very much like the one I had taken only minutes before. It depicted a cramped hallway crudely cut into grey speckled rock. A collection of twisting amber lines crawled across the stone, slightly off center in the frame of the photo. It was a maintenance corridor on an old asteroid mining colony. Lethe Base had been an early contract. I was there investigating a sudden lack of communication from the base. When I arrived I found no settlers, no personal effects, no sign that anybody had ever inhabited the base other than scuffed paint. Everybody just left. The only thing left was that symbol, scrawled on a wall in a seldom used passageway under the center of the compound. There were no signs of violence, no logs of anything having gone wrong. Everything was right where it should have been. Including the ships still docked in the bays. All of them. I checked it when I turned in the report. The company had active lidar scans from before the outpost went quiet to when I arrived on the scene with *Erebus*. No ships had come or gone from the station.

There had been a few others where I had found similar markings, but I hadn't had the opportunity to get photographs of those. There were a few rough sketches I'd made from memory, but nothing perfect. All present at the scenes of strange disappearances, unexplained phenomena, places where the facts just didn't add up. All written off and buried with rationalizations. I glanced at the rest of the files in the locker. There were dozens of them, all strange cases, or cases with no explanation. Most of them were probably apocryphal. Some mentioned strange symbols scrawled on walls or bulkheads at the scene of strange or gruesome tragedies. Most blamed a particularly vicious band of pirates. I had my own reasons to think some of them were legitimate. I also had my own reasons to doubt that those cases were the work of pirates. I contemplated the very real risks of the job. My eyes kept landing on the photos and all the cases that were unexplained and going to stay that way. Realistically, I knew there was no chance I was going to turn around. But I always told myself it was an option.

"I'm going to need Jericho for this," I said to the empty room.

...

After I had stowed the new evidence in the vault, I climbed back to the cockpit and set off along the trail of debris toward whatever was left of the *Alea*. The debris of the ship arced into the infinite emptiness like the ruin of a road between stars.

Or a trail of blood, I thought to myself morbidly.

I kept my hand near the AI's switch at all times. It might have been excessive paranoia if it wasn't completely justified. We sat there in silence as the roadway to our wayward freighter slipped by above us, some of the pieces still polished enough to reflect twinkles of light from *Erebus'* engines and the distant stars. After a lengthy silence, Judas spoke:

"James... Back at that hull fragment. Why didn't you want me to see it? I may have been able to assist you in analyzing the remains."

I scratched my jaw, which reminded me it had been a while since I shaved.

"General paranoia, I suppose."

"Paranoia?" The cool voice asked patiently.

"The first time an AI went screwy on me, I figured it was a freak accident. The second time, I decided I was done taking chances."

"I... See."

We lapsed back into silence then, waiting for the lidar to give us something bigger than a breadbox to work with. After a while I took us to the very edge of the sensor range, told Judas to keep us out as far as we could be without losing the trail, and settled back in the captain's chair to catch up on the sleep I'd lost while we were in subspace.

I don't sleep well. Comes with too much time awake in subspace and too many unpleasant jobs, I guess. I tend to wind up in some of my less pleasant memories when I close my eyes for too long, and this time was no exception...

...

"Harper. Go time."

I roused myself from the light doze I'd slipped into for the transit and blinked around the shuttle's crew compartment. The other members of the boarding team were getting ready in their own idiosyncratic ways. Wilkins was passing his rosary through his hands, praying for the team and the crew of the distressed vessel, and probably his wife and kids too. Sinclair was bobbing his head to some of his weird-but-pretty-good fusion music and checking his go-bag, which was effectively a small hospital you could haul around with you. I stretched and checked my sidearm: retention, safety, safety.

"How far out are we, Artie?" Cobb looked up from his mission pad with a mildly annoyed expression. His rate was Recovery Technician, and he was a first-class patty officer, so in theory Petty Officer Cobb or RT-1 were the correct methods of address. In practice, we all just called the lead Recovery

Technician–RT on any medevac or search and rescue case "Artie".

"Ten mikes," he said distractedly before his gaze dropped back down to the pad. There was a frown on his face.

"Something wrong?" I asked as I moved over to check the CC rig on the wall. That was my job: as a Casualty Control Technician, I was on the mission to patch, plug, weld, shore, or jury rig whatever I could to help the vessel in distress maintain stable orbit or return to a safe port. And technically to provide security for the boarding team, but that was very rarely needed in our quiet, backwater system. Cobb's frown deepened, then he shook his head slightly.

"I don't know. Maybe. We've got them on the scope but their mayday stopped pinging and they're not responding to hails."

I thought for a second as I did final checks on my rig. "Ceecee" Had been painted on the left bicep in flowing script, under a fresh painting depicting a woman wearing a red bandana and a blue shirt flexing her arm. Ceecee was an old but high-quality suit, complete with a powered frame and armor plates to protect against shrapnel, off-gassing, and radiation. I checked the heavy-duty circular saw, the welders and plasma cutters in the fingertips, and the reciprocating saw magazine and rivet feed mounted on the forearms. Everything was topped up, graphite-lubricated, and ready to go. I triple checked the emergency release. The torso and limbs all split cleanly along the emergency seams when I tested them. That was key. The exoskeleton could go from asset to deathtrap if part of it got pinned. slapped the name for luck and went to look over Cobb's shoulder. He briefly glanced at Ceecee before looking back at the screen.

"Thought I told you to repaint that suit," he said in a resigned tone. I adopted a hurt expression.

I adopted a hurt expression.

"But I did, boss. You can actually tell that she's human now."

He glanced at the small painting on the suit.

"I'll grant that it's been upgraded from 'blobs of color' to 'homunculus'. Still out of regs though."

I sighed dramatically.

"Great artists are never appreciated in their time..." I jerked my chin at the display.

"What's going on with this?"

Visually, it just looked like a blue triangle, which represented us, pointing at a red square, which represented the vessel that had sent out the mayday. Vector lines led to and from each, and a timer clicked down at the top of the screen. Curved sepia lines passed through the display in broad arcs, slightly closer at the top left and spreading out. Those showed the gravity well of the nearest celestial body in a kind of topographical map. Lines of text scrolled down either side of the image, new updates to velocities, communications, and a dozen other things.

"Still nothing," Cobb said. He scrolled back through the block of text on the right side of the screen and pointed out one entry.

"That's the last mayday ping we got. If it wasn't for their transponder, we might have lost them. Still no active communication." The entry was time stamped roughly two hours earlier.

"Stopped pinging after we had passed the point of no return," I noted with distaste. "You thinkin' pirates? A four-hundred-footer is a bit big for that." I used the archaic unit without thinking about it and I winced. Cobb hated when I reverted.

He continued to scowl down at the pad as though it would intimidate the technology into showing him the future.

"Use standard units Harper, not mudbug measurements. And not necessarily. Telemetry shows nothing within reach of us, no lidar pings on anything bigger than a couple meters within a six-hour burn. It just seems..."

"Weird?" I finished. He nodded.

"Yeah. Just weird. I'm probably just paranoid. They were already in mayday. There are a million reasons their array might have gone out."

I nodded. Cobb was probably right. It probably was just paranoia. Still, I checked my sidearm again just in case, and I noticed Wilkins doing the same. Security was rarely needed for a search and rescue call. But *rarely* isn't *never*.

...

It came as something of a relief when Judas woke me up.

"James? We seem to have arrived." I swiped the sleep out of my eyes as I replied:

"Seem to have?"

"Your instructions were to remain at the outermost edge of our sensor range. I cannot determine specifics at such a range, but there appears to be a large mass at the edge of our radius. Given the circumstances and approximate size of the object in question, it seems likely we have found the *Alea*, although..." I sat up and peered through the viewport.

"Although?" I asked.

"Its mass and volume metrics are low enough that it could be another object entirely."

That sounded about right. It was too far out to make out any details, but I could see something passing in front of the stars ahead of us. I looked at Judas' main panel.

"Good work, Judas. Ready for a nap?"

20

"I am," he replied. "Do be careful, James. I'm not keen to stay out here with *Alea* forever."

Maybe I would retire this Judas early, send him off to assist the captain of some star yacht back in the Sol system. Hell, maybe I would retire too.

Right. When pigs fly.

I opened Judas' master switch and took the stick. My hand shook a little, but I was still level enough to get the job done. With some trepidation, I eased open the throttle and watched as the speck in the distance slowly grew into a pebble sized object, then a fist, then filled the viewscreen. As the details resolved themselves it became clear that there was more of the ship stretched out behind us than there was left intact. Less than half the ship remained, barely three kilometers left of its original eight. The bow was split and the aft end looked like some temperamental god had grabbed the ship in two hands and simply ripped the aft section away by brute force.

The remains of the ship stretched into the distanced behind me, a trail of cargo pods and hull fragments leading back toward whatever had turned the ship into a wreck. Some gas fires still seemed to be burning along the outside of the hull, which shouldn't have been the case. The *Alea* had gone dark more than two weeks ago. Any fires or gas leaks should have played out by the time I arrived. Then it clicked for me. They weren't gas fires: They were symbols. More glyphs than I'd ever seen in my life. I clenched my hands on the stick. I could list the worst jobs I'd ever worked, and they all had something in common: at least one of

21

those strange symbols. But this was dozens. Dozens, all on the same ship. If there had been any doubt in my mind before that I would need Jericho for this job, it died a brutal death right there. I cruised slowly along the upper surface of the ship, passing over the gaping wound that showed where the vessel had been ripped apart.

Passing over the plates of dull grey metal, something else leaped out at me: the hull was pitted and dimpled, as though chunks of it had simply vanished from existence in some antimatter rainstorm. Up ahead, it looked like the section of the ship that housed the crew was still intact, which was unfortunate. It may have been a callous way to see the situation, but cases where the symbols showed up never have survivors. I only knew of one exception. But since the crew quarters were intact, I was obligated to board the ship and try to find the flight recorder and crew, and in that order of priority. Or at least, that was what I would put on my report. I would check for survivors out of common decency and a sense of professional pride, but I wasn't kicking around dark space out of *agape* love for my fellow man any more than I was doing it out of greed. My gaze stuck on the molten sigils carved into the skin of the *Alea*.

What are you?

That question had been lodged in my brain for over a decade and a half. Almost twenty years of chasing down scraps and rumors, following ghost stories through the deepest shadows in dark space. I had a chance to answer it then. *Alea* had answers. Maybe not all the answers. But answers all the same. My resolve firmed, and I pushed the throttle forward for an approach.

22

I sent a few pings over the short-range radio for the sake of being thorough, but I didn't expect to hear anything back. I'd found bodies on these weird jobs before. Only a few, but still. It's always good to bring people back. But I could count them on one hand. After a while I stopped bringing bodies back from wrecks with the markings on them. I always heard about strange things happening to the people or ships who received them. Somebody would snap, or there would be a freak malfunction. People would die. Nothing that I could ever prove, but eventually I decided discretion would serve the galaxy better than honesty in those cases. The benefit of operating in an inter-system void is that there's no one to gainsay you when you report that there were no recoverable bodies. You do what you have to, and there's no one who's going to send out a second ship to check that the remains were actually unrecoverable. Any ship with a mark I reported as unrecoverable, crew and vessel. It was true enough, and I had learned the hard way that trying to warn anybody directly just meant I wouldn't get any more contracts from that particular system again.

Anyway, I didn't expect to hear anything on the radio, and I didn't. Not at first. But after a few minutes of cruising up the hull and looking for bodies drifting around out there, I noticed that the interference was changing. Not obviously, but there was almost a pattern to what was coming out of the speakers. I checked the star charts and the specifications for the *Alea*, but the kind of slow shifting I was hearing didn't line up with the background radiation or the interference the *Alea* would be generating. I looked at the master control switch for the radio, another hard cutout like Judas' switch. Then I yanked it open. Better safe than sorry, and I had listened long enough to honestly report that no one had been putting out a short-range SOS when I arrived at the scene.

By then I was coming up on the primary airlock, meaning the one located directly behind the bridge, used for most port calls and docking operations. Or, more accurately, the place where the primary boarding airlock would have been. It looked like it had gotten hit with whatever had disintegrated a bunch of the hull. I could actually see into the passageway when I turned on the floodlights.

"Shit." I said flatly.

I thought back to the plans I had studied when I got the job, then consulted with a polymer-sheet map I had printed just to be sure.

"Yep, figures..." I said, nodding to myself. The next best option was three decks down and about five hundred meters back, and would mean that I would have to traverse half the crew deck and the entirety of the command deck to reach the bridge. Not my favorite plan, but the next closest was even more out of the way, so I adjusted my relative speed and spun *Erebus* to line up the topside hatch. I wanted a clear view of what *Alea* was doing from the cockpit if I had to bug out. I sat there for a moment, the ship seeming to loom out over me like a spur of rock jutting over an infinite void, and took a few deep breaths. Then I nodded to myself, thumped Judas' panel, and climbed down to the vault. It was time to gear up.

There are always trade-offs with gear. More equipment means more options, but it also means that you have more weight, more points of failure, and, crucially, more bulk. These things matter if you're operating in confined spaces or in zero gravity, and as you might expect these are common conditions on a derelict cosmo-hauler. My experience with Interdictions and after always led me to the conclusion that less was more. I saw a lot of people get themselves into very bad situations by relying on complicated equipment that was prone to failure in moments of crisis, and too much mass to accelerate—and more importantly, *decelerate*—could get you a broken neck during zero-g maneuvers. I preferred to use simpler, more reliable equipment. There was admittedly less convenience and more work for me that way, but I had very little trust in technology. Particularly after some of my more harrowing encounters with AI.

I selected from my vault my most trusted and reliable equipment: My gun, Jericho, my trusty atomic knife, and, most crucially, my old Bellerophon System Patrol model X-9A vacuum suit.

I wore that suit through every boarding and close call I ever had out in the hard cold, as we called it, and it had never once failed me. It wasn't fancy and didn't have the newest tech, but the CO_2 scrubbers could keep you alive for days on just the internal air supply, the mag boots were smooth and intuitive, and the jet-black carbon nanoweave construction not only eliminated the need for pressurization in most of the suit by applying direct pressure to most of the body, it was thin as a glove and never caught, snagged, or tore. The suit's range of motion was customized to exactly mimic mine, making dislocation or hyperextension of joints extremely difficult, though it was still possible. The nanoweave locked up under impact and spread any force evenly across most of my body, meaning I was more resilient to falls or collisions. It was a beautiful, simple, marvel of engineering. Looking at the opaque visor of the sleek, low-profile helmet always filled me with confidence. That smooth sheet of dully reflective, gunmetal grey carbon matrix had kept me alive through more vacuum exposure than most people ever saw.

I briefly considered suiting up in the Casualty Control suit, but maneuverability is paramount in zero g, especially on a derelict. The priority was to be able to get out of the ship as fast as possible, for any number of reasons. A couple hundred kilos of metal exoskeleton and tools made that fairly difficult, and it would take power to run it, cutting into my suit reserves and survival time. I decided to travel light. I wasn't trying to repair or salvage *Alea*, I was investigating it. If I found any casualties big enough to warrant the suit, I would be bugging out. In that situation, maneuvering three hundred kilos of mass in zero g would be a nightmare: CC suits don't have thrusters.

Jericho had won me more than one fight. Jericho was an old-school capacitor actuated mass-driver pistol, meaning you had to manually load a cartridge containing the tungsten alloy mass slug and a miniaturized, ultra-high-storage capacitor and actuate it with a mechanical trigger. Pulling the trigger would release a hammer which would complete the circuit and allow the discharge of the capacitor's charge. That power was used simultaneously in the mass driver and a simple recoil dampener. The second part was necessary because without it, Jericho would shatter the limb of anyone who was either brave enough or dumb enough to fire it. The raiders who designed it had based the design of the pistol on old Terran revolvers, albeit scaled up a bit. Their cylinders and single action triggers had unparalleled reliability in austere combat, particularly in extreme low-temperature conditions where more complex loading and firing mechanisms were prone to failure. The design also allowed each round to pack an astonishing amount of power. The trade-off was that each cartridge was, by modern standards, gargantuan, and ammunition was both expensive and bulky. It was also highly illegal in virtually every system humans had settled. It was a good trade. With the additional dozen rounds on Jericho's gun belt and holster, I had exactly eighteen rounds. I had once used the weapon to blow myself an exit through the outer hull of a derelict. Bringing eighteen rounds was probably overkill.

The atomic knife, despite the name, is not powered by atomic energy. It is in fact not powered at all. The name comes from the fact that an atomic knife's edge is less than an atom wide, and the blade isn't a great deal wider. The only way to make something like that is to create it from a neutron matrix known as neutronium. I always wondered how it was made and how they accounted for the absolutely staggering density of neutronium. Even aside from the fact that my knife should realistically weigh more than several planets, neutronium was notoriously unstable, prone to dissociating rapidly without immense gravitational forces. How the feat had been achieved, and why, was a lost secret. Nobody knew exactly who made the few neutronium tools and weapons we'd found, or when. I only had one because I had investigated a missing ship that was moving rare antiquities and I "salvaged" the knife while I was exploring the wreck. The benefits of this construction involve being able to cut through any mundane matter with ease, and being indestructible. Whoever made mine had made it in the style of balisong, an extremely old design consisting of a blade and two handles attached by swiveling pins in such a manner that the handles, when closed, cover the edges of the knife like a sheath. I suspect it was the only way they could think to contain the edge. It had a special spot on my custom holster for Jericho, which kept both of my most trusted weapons close to my hand at all times. I gave the knife a few flicks of my wrist, spinning the ebony handles apart and revealing the absolute, perfect black of the blade, then flicked it shut and slipped it into its spot at my hip with an affectionate pat.

A few other odds and ends went on my belt or into a bag I liked to wear at my side, where it could be easily ditched: a crowbar, a couple canisters of water, a spool of fry-wire, my magnetic grapple, and spare copies of maps and briefings on the *Alea*. I had memorized as much of that documentation as I could, but even a trained memory is writing in sand at the best of times, and I like to be sure about things. As I sealed up my helmet and did a final triple check of all my gear, I took a few deep breaths, and nodded to myself. *Go time.*

Chapter Four

If you've ever been alone in an old house, you know that there's a weird sense of unease you get when you're in an abandoned, man-made structure. I think it's something about the way it's clearly *made* to have people in it, and just as clearly *doesn't.* It's worse on ships. The thought of something that was built to bring freedom, exploration, trade, becoming a tomb drifting through the cold dark is just... wrong. Stepping through the airlock of the *Alea* filled me with that eerie feeling, just like it always does on wrecks. The first thing I saw when the doors *whooshed* apart on their own emergency power was a dark grey corridor, hexagonal just like the hull of the ship. It was pitch black except for the lamp on my helmet, which cut a cold white swathe through the murk, sparkling off of shards of metal and dust in the air. Panels had been torn off the bulkheads and wires, conduit, and insulation were drooping out like bizarre ferns. Even before the wreck, it looked like *Alea* had lived a hard life. The deck and bulkheads were dull and scratched, marred by too much hard use and too little maintenance. Before I took a step, I flicked on my helmet's loudspeaker and took a breath.

"Ahoy, crew of the *Alea.*"

I spoke calmly, but my voice boomed out of the speaker, echoing off the strange geometry of the bulkheads and bouncing back distorted. I shifted my satchel back and called again.

"James Harper, Harper Investigations. I've been contracted to find and determine the state of your vessel. I'm here under contact with the Hwong-Howell Corporation."

Nothing. Onboard a cosmo-hauler, the law of its system of registry is technically in effect, so I was required to announce myself to the crew when boarding, should they be present. The crew, however, was notable by its absence. There weren't any calls back, but I checked the crew registry I'd printed on a sheet of polymer. Sixty-three crew, ranging from an old duster named Thom Wilks to a seventeen-year-old kid named Isaac Bly. I also had a list of distinguishing features for each crew member to aid in identification of the deceased, but that wouldn't help much. About the most useful thing on there was that the kid had a tattoo of a fish on his forearm. Not terribly useful if all I had to go on was a leg or part of a torso, which was frequently the case in my line of work. After waiting about thirty seconds, I nodded to myself and started picking my way down the passageway.

There was detritus strewn all about the deck, food containers and bits of rubbish that had no clear reason for being there. I kept my right hand on the grip of my trusty pistol, and one eye on the readout on my left arm. That rig was the only computer I would bring with me onto a wreck, and that was because it had no direct control over my suit's life support systems and I didn't absolutely need it to survive. It showed in simple red vector graphics the schematics for *Alea*, the backup listing of the crew, current radiation levels, power fluctuations, and various atmospheric readings which currently indicated that the air was breathable, but the CO_2 scrubbers and filters seemed to have been offline for quite some time. It looked like several of the ship's auxiliary power systems were still active, which explained why there was still artificial gravity on this deck. Looked like zero g in a lot of it though.

I followed my rudimentary map of the ship towards the nearest ladder up, which seemed to be located on the far side of the galley. I went warily through the darkness. There are few places less safe than a shipwreck of unknown cause. The reactor could have been cooking over since *Alea* went missing a week ago, getting ready to blow. The hull may have been corroded or weakened and be getting ready to blow me out into infinity, there could be debris my docking and movement through the ship would knock loose, the crew might be in a hysterical state of panic after a week drifting off course without the half of their ship that had the engines in it, any number of things. A good investigator takes things slowly and engages in a certain amount of professional cowardice. If things start to go south you get the hell out of there before you're just another corpse on the deep freeze.

They say never to speak ill of the dead, but I couldn't help but admonish the crew of the *Alea* internally. The poor girl's keel had only been laid about twenty years ago, but the interior looked like something that had gone forty or fifty years without preventative maintenance, not a cosmo-hauler in the prime of her career. I started to wonder if the torn away bulkheads and garbage on the floor were a result of the crash, or the cause of it. It looked like the crew had been panicking and burning through their food stores too fast on top of it.

There was no way they should have gone through this much in such a short time. I understood the fear of being adrift in the sea of stars--all too well, if I'm honest--but they should have been better trained than that. As I moved through the ship, it felt more like exploring some ancient and undiscovered cave system than it did moving through what had recently been a spacefaring vessel. At every intersection the crossing passageways loomed like gaping maws, filled with inky darkness like mineshafts. As I swept my light across one such intersection, I saw that one section of corrosion was so bad the entire panel looked brown with rust from the deck to about the halfway point up the bulkhead. Then I stopped and looked back. I hadn't seen any corrosion that bad on the interior of the ship and that color... I took a few steps forward and knelt down to bring my light as close as possible to the discoloration.

Blood? It was an old bloodstain. A very, very old bloodstain.

From someone who got thrown into the bulkhead when the ship fragmented?

No, that didn't seem likely. There wasn't much on the deck, and no marks where they would have been pulled out of the puddle. No drag marks or spatter around the edge of the stain. I flipped the retention strap on and off my pistol while I thought. That stain could have come from the incident that damaged the ship. On the other hand, if it hadn't then someone had caused it. Maybe boarders--pirates--or crew on crew violence. Either option was unpleasant to contemplate. The smart thing to do would be to bug out of here, log the *Alea* as having collided with an object of unknown nature and size, and collect the slightly smaller check that meant I hadn't returned a full report or AI core. Not that I would risk bringing a contaminated and damaged AI core onboard *Erebus* in any case. Or handing it off to the company.

I checked my map. It was a circuitous route to the bridge, where I could locate the primary flight recorder. If that failed, I would have to go all the way down to Engineering and improvise heavily. The bridge was about five hundred meters fore of my current position, and it was almost a full kilometer down to Engineering, which was directly above the keel of the ship. That was lot longer than I really wanted to go on a potentially unstable derelict if I was honest with myself. The exterior of the bridge had been intact, but there was no way to know if the interior was still reachable, or if the flight recorder itself was intact.

I could have left. Nobody would know, and nobody would blame me. Most would probably think I was stupid for setting foot on a derelict at all. I could leave, and *Alea* would become just another one of those strange cases, filed away and eventually forgotten about. Unexplained and buried. I thought of my box on *Erebus* full of cases like this one, cases where nobody had answers and nobody was looking for them. And old memory brushed against the back of my mind. I clenched my hand around my pistol's grip and kept walking.

It only took me maybe another five minutes to get to the galley, and I noticed the lack of apparent maintenance was getting more pronounced. Here, even portions of the deck plating had been torn up for some reason I couldn't ascertain. The deck plates themselves were nowhere to be seen. A lot of things weren't adding up here. The lights had been cut to this whole quarter, but the auxiliary power systems on a ship this size could keep essential systems running for something like fifty years, and the artificial gravity was still active. From the missing plates it seemed like the crew had taken them somewhere else, but I couldn't think what use the thin, low strength alloy would be for any damage control or emergency repairs.

Patching the hull, maybe?

That didn't make any sense. *Alea's* hull was more than a meter thick in most places. I stepped into the mess deck and what I saw made me glad I was wearing a vacuum suit. Food stains smeared the walls, along with what looked like more blood. Wrappers for prepackaged emergency rations littered the floor, and containers for the kind of ready-made meals that busy people ate too often were fuzzed over with mold. There had clearly been a shootout. The tables had been cut off the floor and stacked against the far hatch in a rudimentary barricade, but they were blasted through and pocked with what had clearly been gunfire. The hatch looked like it had been forced inward by brute strength, three inches of solid metal crumpled like foil. Wrappers and containers crunched and rustled as I crossed the room. Fungus spores puffed up with each step, clouds of fine particles stirring into eddies in my wake.

I clambered over the bent metal, careful not to snag anything on the jagged edge of the torn door. The galley itself wasn't in better shape. Bullet holes and more bloodstains. Every implement that could potentially be used for violence was either gone or covered in dried blood. Looked like someone had smashed up a good few of the maintenance bots too, just to be thorough.

Maybe someone weaponized the drones?

I couldn't wrap my head around the scene. One of the cooktops had the kind of suspicious charring that looked like it might be from someone being forced onto it while it was still hot. Blood was painted up the walls and splattered on the overhead.

Fucking hell...

I spotted the bloody shards of what had clearly been a glass coffeepot. Whatever happened here was beyond fucked.

I wasn't keen on wandering around what was likely still a war zone, but luckily it wasn't far to the ladder well. I drew my pistol and reminded myself that I had signed on for this willingly. I dimmed my lamp to a much more subtle glow and moved cautiously into the corridor behind the galley, smoothly placing one foot in front of the other just like they taught us in boarding school.

It was only about twenty or so meters from the galley to the maintenance ladder, but there was something different in this section of the ship. It had started in the galley, but as I progressed further I felt my heart rate rise. A sense of pressure settled in around my body. The compartments I passed all seemed to have... Misplaced their hatches. They looked like they had been ready rooms, spaces for storing food between hauling it up from the storeroom and prepping it. A couple were full of rags and old clothes ripped up and piled up like rodent nests. One held some empty food containers. The last one in the row was full of feces, a mound of waste as high as my thighs. On the wall opposite the door, in hand-wide strokes, someone has used excrement to draw a glyph. My hand clamped down on the grip of Jericho. I had a sudden conviction that my search for survivors was futile.

The one thing none of the compartments contained, at all as far as I could see, was food. I couldn't understand how the crew could have burned through the stores that quickly. They had been under way for quite some time, but their last port call had been roughly two weeks ago. It just didn't add up unless they had dispensed with all rationing and simply gorged themselves constantly. Even then... I shook my head as I stared at the glyph on the far bulkhead of the compartment. Then I turned and kept walking.

I almost walked by the recessed ladder, I was so busy checking up and down the corridor, but my elbow clipped the upright as I walked past. I looked up at the hatch for the ladder, which should have been sealed, but it was another yawning mouth into a dark tunnel. I only had to go up three decks to get the same level as the bridge, but stuffing yourself into a confined space on a derelict is usually a bad idea.

Not like I have all that many options...

I was roughly in the center of the ship and getting to the nearest lift would be a couple hundred meters of extra maneuvering through the wreck. Definitely a worse idea than a quick ladder trip.

I looked up and down the hallway one more time, back to the galley, then the other way, deeper into the ship and towards the engineering spaces. Seeing nothing, I turned back to the ladder, but something made me whip around, pistol lined up for a shot. Something had crossed the next intersection as I had turned. I was sure of it. I flicked on my helmet's speaker, a little less loud than last time:

"Captain James Harper of the *Erebus* and Harper Investigations. If you're crew, you are required to present yourself. Your ship has been designated lost in transit and I am under contract with the owner to investigate the reason for your lack of communication. Noncompliance may result in physical injury to your person or persons."

Nothing.

Shy, are we?

I felt my unease transform into excitement. I talked to an old boxer once. He said no matter how many times he fought, or how many times he won, he always had the jitters until the fight started. I'm no different. I hate the period before things go to shit more than when they actually do. It's the waiting, not knowing how things will go wrong, not having any information to inform a decision.

But now I knew something. Something else was in here. I prowled forward with my pistol at the ready. I paused, gun held low, at the corner, listening for movement and checking the opposite side of the hallway. Then I leaned into the corner and swung around, gun up.

"Show yourself! Incident investigator!"

I was looking down the sights at... another empty passageway. Trashed like the rest, continuing for at least twenty meters without any doors or intersections. There was no way anyone was moving that distance in the time it had taken me to clear the corner, without making noise. I checked the other branches of the intersection, but they were the same. Nothing but rubbish, stains, and the odd missing panel. I narrowed my eyes at the darkness.

Head games. Every time.

I didn't have time to clear the whole damn ship, not that it was even possible with just one person, so I kept my head on a swivel and backtracked to the ladder. Then I scaled the ladder and entered the maintenance tube with an uncomfortable sensation of being swallowed. The tube was a claustrophobe's nightmare. My back rubbed against the metal all the way up, and I had to awkwardly slide my hands past my chest to move them up a rung.

The rungs had bloody hand prints every now and then, the brown almost black in the red lamp from my helmet. I kept an ear out for movement, but my reluctant host was nowhere to be heard. I hauled my way up to the command deck, which contained the bridge. Just past the operations deck, I stopped. I could have sworn... I moved my helmet to touch the side of the maintenance tube, then jerked it back slightly. Something was moving in there. Skittering around like a rat on an old wooden galley. Maybe several somethings. It sounded like maintenance bots, the little cat sized drones that usually handled the most minor repairs on a ship this big.

I sped up my pace, moving as quickly as I could up the cramped ladder. I wasn't terribly afraid, but that tube was the last place I wanted to have some malfunctioning robot decide I was an obstruction that needed a good dose of the old laser cutter. I made it the rest of the way to the command deck without being lasered into pieces, but the exit hatch of the maintenance tube was seized shut. It took practiced application of the crowbar I carry in my satchel for just his reason to force the dogs open without creating a racket fit to wake the dead. It was the kind of job that would have been easy if I hadn't been in a cramped little tube standing with one foot on the rungs of the ladder, one on the threshold of the door, continually looking down between my feet and craning my head back to look up to make sure I wasn't about to get ripped apart by the robotic equivalent of rodents.

Eventually, though, the final dog swung out of place and I was able to shove the door open by bracing my back against the tube and pushing it open with one leg. It squealed horribly, but there wasn't much I could do about that and I needed to get out of there to get the job done, so I just called it the cost of doing business. After a few more good shoves, there was enough of a gap for me to slip out, pistol held ready in case my little buddy followed me up here. I cleared the passageway both ways, then knelt down with my back to a wall and consulted my map. I only had a couple turns to go to get to the bridge. One way or another, that would give me some insight into whatever the hell was happening here. I folded the map back up and slipped it into a thigh pocket of my suit, then froze when something caught my eye. There was something written on the bulkhead behind me:

THEY HAVE THE BRIDGE

I couldn't tell what it was written with, as it was just too chipped and faded. At that point I was just grateful that it wasn't blood. At the least, a picture was forming: The *Alea* had been boarded by pirates, and the crew had tried to hold them off. There were still some oddities there though. Pirates rarely went after anything as big as *Alea*; it was hard to move and offload this much cargo, for one thing, and it was sure to invite reprisals for the loss of such a major investment. Sieges weren't their MO either, too risky. But *something* had kept the crew holed up and burning through rations.

Unless this happened after the wreck, instead of the other way around.

That was a distasteful thought. Intersystem law is a loose shackle when a freighter like this probably never got closer than a few thousand kilometers to any given space station or planet. Things could have been approaching a boil for a while now, maybe even an ongoing turf war between different factions of the crew. It would be neither the first nor the last of such occurrences in the millions of cosmo-hauler plying the ways between stars, if that were the case.

Maybe the pirates got trapped on the Alea? Things escalate, someone takes control of the sub-drive for leverage, someone tries to take it back...

That could work. It didn't fit perfectly, but it could work. I suspected stranger things had happened here. There was still so much missing though. I rifled through my satchel left-handed and snapped a quick picture of the writing. I stuck the photo in its case without waiting to see if it had been a good shot or not. That camera wasn't strictly for business. It was more for my own satisfaction than anything.

My evidence safely stowed, I turned back toward the bow of the ship, and the bridge thay lay there. The ladder had deposited me in a T-intersection, the primary passageway running from fore to aft, and the other athwartships. I checked my map. Main passageway was the shortest route. Or it would have been. I had only taken a step or two towards it when my lamp illuminated something unexpected: the emergency vacuum shutters were down. Not every passageway on a ship has such things, because thirty-centimeter-thick pieces of metal simply aren't practical for every passageway. They mostly served to divide the operations and crew decks into sections in the event of decompression, preventing the entire crew from being spaced if the hull was punctured.

I could get through this one, but I had no way of knowing if it was hard cold on the other side and I only had so much fry-wire. I consulted my map. My best guess was that I was seeing the result of the missing main airlock. The port branch of the passageway, to my left, would take me right into vacuum and I would run into the same problem I was having here.

Starboard it is...

I turned to my right. The passageway stretched out in front of me like pit I was staring into from a great height. My lamp seemed like it wasn't cutting the darkness quite as well as it should. I felt my hackles go up, and I drew Jericho.

Decompression be damned.

I prowled forward at a combat walk, the steady, almost seated posture and gait one uses when prioritizing steady shooting. Someone was here. I just didn't know who, or why they would be hiding from me. There were many more compartments in this section of the ship, each with its own role to play in the proper running of the ship. Most were crew staterooms, two- or three-man berths. Some were for logisticians who managed the onload, organization, and offload of cargo at the appropriate times, some were for engineers who would generally monitor the engines from here and ride the internal monorail eight clicks, or four now, if they needed to actually repair anything back at the engines. There were others for every varied task that arose in the course of *Alea's* operations. They were all in the same state of disarray that I now considered to be the norm for *Alea*: hatches were missing from their frames, and it looked like someone had taken everything from the compartments that wasn't welded down, then come back with a plasma saw and taken everything that *was* welded down, too. There were far more bullet holes on this deck than I had seen so far on the ship.

There were three more passageways that should have led forward from the transverse corridor I was now in, at least according to my map, but teach time I came abreast of them, I found them blocked. One was sealed with another emergency shutter, likely forced closed. Someone had obviously tried to cut through it. There was a long scorch mark from the deck up to about chest height. It was directly over a bloodstain. The other two explained where some of the furniture and cladding had gone: they were barricaded with piles of junk metal that had been crudely fixed together. Sometimes by primitive welds, other times by virtue of various pieces of metal being twisted around each other. I considered going through these as well, but from the gaps in them it looked like they had made up for the lack of strength with volume, the corridors seemingly full of flotsam and metal for several meters. Eventually I reached the end of the athwartships corridor and found myself at another T-junction.

The right led apparently to the docking and service bays for the maintenance drones. Nothing for me there. The left was my way to the bridge and I took it without hesitation. Something was odd about this corridor. I only moved three or four meters before I realized what it was. It was a kill box. I had expected something like this. There was a barricade at the end of my lamp's reach, slightly indistinct in the glimmer of dust and metal particles in the too-dirty atmosphere. There were a number of vertical gashes in it.

Murder holes.

I took cover behind the corner again, just in case. It was quite literally a medieval tactic. In the days of castle and siege warfare, the approach to the castle and keep would be made as long and circuitous as possible, and the route lined with crenelations at the top of the wall and murder holes in the main body of the walls. The murder holes served as ports that enabled rocks, arrows, and sometimes human excrement or boiling liquid to be thrown down on attackers, without exposing the defenders to retaliation. Someone had established this passageway to be a meat grinder. From that distance, attempting to retaliate against the defenders or advance through the corridor was suicide, unless you had... well, unless you had Jericho. Or something bigger. That made sense if the crew were in fact fighting for control of the ship. The bridge and engineering would be two of the key control points for any pirates to seize if they wanted to be able to move the ship and see where they were going while they did it.

I took a breath and thought for a moment. I generally operate under the assumption that everyone and everything on a wreck is trying to kill me. It's only paranoia if it doesn't happen. They could simply be too afraid to interact with me, which...

Unlikely,

I thought as I eyed another blood stain, or they could simply think it would be better to wait to attack. Which would mean I was playing directly into their hands by going deeper into the ship, effectively committing suicide by moving into a prepared position alone and under gunned. Damn. But I'd signed a contract, and in that contract I agreed to make every reasonable effort to ascertain the reason for *Alea's* loss and recover any survivors. And given that I was only a couple hundred meters from the bridge, I knew I hadn't made that effort. Not yet. Nor had a really learned anything new.

The only way out is through, I reminded myself.

I swallowed my unease and forged ahead. I slipped around the corner with Jericho at the ready, keying my helmet's loudspeaker:

"Ahoy crew of the *Alea.* James Harper, Harper Investigations. Present yourselves for rescue if you are able! If you are unable, announce your presence however you can and I will assist you!"

Nothing.

I marched towards the barricade with my right hand on Jericho, ready to use the fast draw I had perfected over more than a decade of practice, but not overtly threatening. My eyes were on the barricade while my peripheral vision monitored the hatches I passed. Most were welded shut. Some looked like they had been partially torn open, but there was nothing I could get through. As I went, the passageway seemed to deteriorate until I was stepping on bare cables more often than actual deck plates. Every now and then I'd hear the skittering of one of the maintenance drones, but there was something oddly arrhythmic about it. If I had to guess, I'd say most of the little buggers were wandering around without a full complement of legs. I didn't like that they hadn't shown themselves. I should have seen more than a few scuttling around

on errands by now, and the fact that they were active but...
reclusive... didn't ease my mind at all.

Creeping through the jagged, dismantled passageway felt
like crawling into the mouth of some monstrosity from the depths
of the sea. Every step ratcheted my nerves tighter. Approaching
the barricade was most likely suicidally stupid. If I spooked some
hungry, exhausted, traumatized deckhand, I'd either be Swiss
cheese or I'd have to blow the whole thing to kingdom come with
Jericho and hope for the best. The passageway ran probably
about two thirds of the distance to the bridge, and I was eminently
aware of what a long way that was to go without decent cover.
Forty meters. More blood stains. They were only getting thicker.
Thirty meters. More bullet holes. Twenty meters. Cables were
hanging from the overhead like vines in a bizarre metal jungle.
Ten. There were virtually no decks or bulkheads to speak of now,
they had been shredded by what was clearly small arms fire. Five.
I could see it clearly now.

Up close, it was clear that the barricade was abandoned.
There were bloodstains right on the mash of metal, which seemed
to be made up mostly of torn off hatches and deck plating. It was
fairly solid, and there were no real gaps other than the murder
holes. I shone my lamp through cautiously, peeking like a child
would around a door jamb. It looked like... another barricade.
Maybe three or four meters behind the first. I didn't see murder
holes though. No sign of hostiles. My right hand flicked my a-
knife open with a satisfying snick-snick-clack, and I carved into
the edge of one of the murder holes with the nano-scale edge. For
things like this the slender, hand-length blade was perfect. It didn't
take long before there was a pile of metal scraps at my feet and I

was able flick my knife closed in a smooth movement and climb through, hand on Jericho.

The purpose of the second barricade was immediately clear. It sealed of the corridor completely, forcing me to take a left turn, towards the center of the ship. there was a short corridor leading into what should be...

The rec deck?

I wasn't sure why they would want to force the attackers through the recreational area, but this defense was clearly well thought out. They would likely have another position set up in there somewhere.

But is there anyone left to man it?

I crossed the short passageway and stacked up on the door. I huffed a non-laugh.

Not much of a stack with just one...

Times like these were where I questioned working solo. I knew I couldn't take the risk on a crew, but damn if it wouldn't be nice to have a crew watching my back just then.

I'm a fucking idiot, I thought.

I knew that, but still. Good to keep it fresh. I drew Jericho and angled the gunmetal visor of my helmet at the doorway to direct the sound of my hail:

"Attention, crew of the *Alea*. Captain James Harper, Harper Investigations. Your vessel has been designated lost in transit by the Hwong-Howell Corporation. Present yourselves for evacuation and debrief."

I heard it echo. I switched off the speaker.

"Or not..." I muttered to myself. I waited a tick, then pied the corner and sidestepped out of the doorway. Silhouettes are the most common shape for target practice for good reason: They're easy to identify and acquire as targets, so it's usually smart to avoid presenting one if you can. I scanned the room as I swept through that arc and sidestep, Jericho at the low ready.

It was a round room maybe twenty-five meters across, roughly divided into thirds. One third was dedicated to a rather impressive weight room, equaling even the equipment I kept on *Erebus*. Another was devoted to a viewscreen and various simulation consoles, along with some bookshelves on one wall. The last was dedicated to various game tables and competitions. Billiards, table tennis, darts, and especially card tables. The vice of sailors since time immemorial. Rummy had been the game of choice among my crew. Why was anyone's guess. Everything was broken, scattered. There were bloodstains, bullet holes, and signs of conflict everywhere. Dumbbells crusted with blood on one end. Console cables that had snapped. Garrotes? Restraints? No way to know. Pool cues had been sharpened into stakes and clearly used to some effect.

The feeling was overwhelmingly that of having disturbed an ancient tomb, left untouched for generations and now

48

desecrated by a looter. The yellowed pages of the books and the thick dust blanketing the wrecked pieces of furniture showed the passage of time.

Seeing the rec deck bothered me. It's hard to explain but they're almost sacred. You're locked up in a can with people you might not like on a ship, but the rec deck is a place where everyone can relax and blow off steam, kill time and take their minds off the birthdays, anniversaries, and sometimes even funerals they're missing. It's a lonely kind of life in a lot of ways, making your way between the stars. You get to see parts of the galaxy no one else does, but you have no anchor to keep you steady. Freedom comes at a price. Seeing the evidence of carnage in a place meant to be a haven for these poor bastards... to me it was the most unsettling thing yet. It just didn't belong here. There were four entrances to the large compartment, fore, aft, port, and starboard. I had entered through the starboard hatch. The port and aft had both been welded over with more of the deck plates and hatches that had gone missing, and there were the remains of what looked like a sort of pillbox built around the forward hatch.

The port barricade, however, had clearly been blown in somehow. I cautiously circled around the aft arc of the room to inspect the port hatch. It had been blown in, but there was something odd about it. I stared, trying to place it place it until--

No heat.

I realized there were no scorch marks. No melted edges of metal or liquified plastic like I would expect if explosives had done this. I was intimately familiar with the results of using such things within ships, and this wasn't demo work. It was...

Brute force.

Someone had hauled a mech or something else big up here and just battered their way through the hatch. I looked across the room at the forward hatch and the remains of the gun position in front of it.

And then they just kept going... Maybe one of the loaders? They could have been shipping heavy equipment.

I looked back to the makeshift fortification. It was solid, or had been anyway. Whatever had come through here had pushed through it like cardboard, and then kept going right through the next checkpoint. Cleverly designed defenses don't mean much when the enemy can simply knock your walls over like they're made of wooden blocks. I carefully slipped through the scattered debris, crossing the room to the forward hatch. As my gaze traced over the bloodstains there, another thing bothered me. There was just too much blood.

At a rough estimate of four or five liters of blood in a single body, the fact that I had been seeing stains throughout the entire ship just didn't add up without the addition of more people. Pirates were increasingly likely culprits. I passed through the hatch and into another short, connecting corridor. There were only two side compartments, one on either side of the passage. One was a smallish room, almost a booth, that was clearly the comm booth for the q-graph. Quantum telegraphs use pairs of entangled particles to transmit messages by altering the spin of one, say here on the ship. That would in turn alter the spin of paired particle, probably at Hwong-Howell headquarters. This allowed instant communication regardless of distance. The method used was actually one of the oldest communications tools around: Morse code. Two particles flipping between spin states don't have the bandwidth to really transmit information in computer code at reasonable speed and managing multiple particles is unnecessarily complicated, so telegraphers use the historical code to exchange information directly. I hear they're figuring out how to do it with computers, but I like to know there's a soul on the other end of the line. *Alea's* q-graph had been obliterated. Why anyone would destroy her only means of calling for help was a question with only bad answers. There wasn't a piece left bigger than my hand.

The room across the way looked like it had been the gun locker. Most ships keep a gun locker to repel pirates; simply arming the crew during routine operations isn't usually the best idea. The hatch had been cut through and emptied, every rifle, pistol, round, and knife long, long gone. I surveyed the empty compartment, then turned and looked down the passageway. It was time to investigate the bridge.

Chapter Five

As I looked at the hatch into the bridge, I found myself with something of a mystery on my hands. Almost every hatch on this entire deck of the ship had been cut away and carted off to who knows where or used in the make shift defenses. Almost every hatch. The hatch to the bridge was still here. Dented, scorched, and pockmarked, yes. But present, and with no sign of cutting taking place. Plenty of shooting, but no distinctive marks from plasma saws or lasers. Not even any soot from old oxy-acetylene cutters. The bridge, as far as I could tell, was still sealed up like a can of tuna. The problem now became how to get through a door specifically designed to be a last-ditch holdout against pirates and mutineers. None of the manual overrides or salvage codes provided in the information about the ship were effective; it was jammed from the inside. No conventional way in, which meant that I'd have to use a tool that Sinclair would have called crude: fry-wire

The enterprising pirates that lurk at the edges of the inhabited systems are innovators par excellence when it comes to circumventing security systems, and a few years back I'd picked up a favorite toy from one of their derelicts: a little something they call "fry-wire". To the naked eye it's a spool of heavy gauge wire the size of your palm, unremarkable to every mundane sense. It has one hell of a trick though: I'm not sure what exactly it's made of, but I know it involves a lot of combustible metals and it burns hotter than hell. Hot enough to, say, cut through six inches of reinforced hatch. It's also highly illegal in every settled star system due to its volatile nature, but operating between settled star systems affords me certain liberties with that kind of thing.

I pulled a spool of fry-wire off my belt and laid out the main "doorway" that I would use to access the space, then laid out a small circle about as big around as my thumb and index finger in an "ok" sign. The small circle was a trick I learned the hard way, after nearly venting myself into space once: You always cut a hole small enough to plug first, just to see whether there's hard vacuum on the other side. I lit off the test cut and watched it slowly burn through the metal in a rough circle, all the way up until it... Fizzled out and left a circle of glowing, semi-molten metal behind. That was good. if there was vacuum on the other side of that hatch, then as soon as the fry-wire cut through the metal, the plug would have been shot into the bridge like a pellet from an air rifle. The fact that it stayed in place meant that there was enough atmosphere on the other side of the bridge to roughly equalize with the corridor in which I stood.

Once the second string of wire was lit, I had a couple of minutes to kill, so I did a quick sweep of the bridge wings. On an old seafaring ship, the bridge wings would have been exposed to the air, but in the cosmonautical age they've become docking points for lifeboats; small craft that will keep the crew alive at least a little while longer in the event a vessel goes down. Most were built as part of the ship and would blow free if necessary, and *Alea's* was no different. On a ship her size, the lifeboat likely had a sub-drive of its own, albeit one that could only do short hops.

Alea's lifeboat had been sabotaged. The controls had been hacked to pieces. There were holes cut in the hull and conduits and components had been cut to pieces. I stood there for a moment, one hand clenched into a fist and the other locked on the grip of Jericho.

Fucking savages.

I knew better than most just how bad abandoning ship with nothing but your suit could be. Whoever the fuck was left on this sorry can would be answering a lot of questions before they went anywhere on *Erebus*. If they'd had anything to do with this, they'd be riding *Alea* all the way to the end of the line.

It didn't make sense. Even the most vicious mutineer wants one person to get off the ship alive: himself. A quick count showed that even the lifeboat's compliment of emergency vacuum suits had been destroyed. They were all present and rendered useless. Destroying the suits wasn't an act of mutiny; it was a combination murder/suicide. It was something you did if you didn't want anybody getting off the ship alive.

Pirates? I thought to myself again.

Maybe. But then why not call for help? Why destroy the q-graph?

No matter how fast the pirates were, there was no way they could overrun the crew fast enough that they couldn't get a call out on the q-graph. Besides, the makeshift fortifications spoke to a drawn-out conflict, something I could scarcely believe fit in the two weeks *Alea* had been missing. It didn't figure. It was illogical. Pirates might have scuttled the ship after looting it or if they couldn't take it but... They almost certainly wouldn't engage in the kind of prolonged conflict indicated by the evidence. Mutineers wouldn't want to kill themselves as well as the officers, and would have a vested interest in keep the ship as intact as they could. None of it added up to anything that made sense. I thought of the glyphs covering the hull and scattered throughout the ship, and the rock in my stomach got a little heavier. Something was deeply, deeply wrong here.

When the fry-wire finished cutting through the hatch, I was ready. I stood there drumming my fingers on the grip of my pistol, warily eyeing the athwartships passage and the route I had taken to get there. I kicked the plate through the hatch with a bit more force than was probably necessary. Silhouetted against the darkness of the bridge, the glowing edges of the metal seemed like a portal right into subspace.

A doorway into an event horizon...

With that cheery thought, I slipped through the hole, pistol out in case of any jumpy survivors. I didn't find any. What I did find was a lot more very old bloodstains. It took me a quarter hour to figure out what had happened, and at least some of the missing panels made a little more sense now. There were dozens of small holes cut through the deck plates and bulkhead cladding of the bridge. The edges were the distinct, perfect cuts you only get from a laser. Hundreds of tiny tracks spiraled through the blood stains, covering the deck, bulkheads, and overhead with dotted lines like a macabre, abstract painting. Whoever had holed up here hadn't had control of the bots. They'd been sent in through the conduit runs and butchered everyone on the bridge. I looked at the hatch behind me; it had been welded shut from the inside.

"What the hell happened to you people?" I asked the shadows.

Equally unsettling was the fact that there were no visible bodies, in whole or in part, on the entire bridge. Or anywhere else. It had been bugging me ever since I found the first signs of violence. I could believe that the last holdouts may have spaced the rest of the crew and then repressurized the ship, but they should still be here. Eyeing the obvious egress points into the bridge, and considering the fact that it was still pressurized, I had to conclude that they had been removed by the bots after death.

Why?

I picked my way across the deck, avoiding the blood where I could, to the nav console. The local copy of the flight recorder, on any ship of any affiliation, is located on the nav console to allow the Navigations Officer to grab it in the event of an evacuation. Alternately, the recovery team or agent will know where to look for it, if said officer is missing or deceased. I knelt down to unlatch the cover, and paused. I sighed, briefly and with some justification, I think. It was turning into that kind of day. Grinning at me below the nav console, conspicuously empty, was the slot for the flight recorder's bridge copy.

What that meant was that I now had to go all the way down to Engineering, where the ship's massive processors and data banks crunched and stored enormous amounts of information. The good news was that Engineering was in the surviving portion of the ship. The bad news was that the damage to the main deck had rendered the simplest route there nonviable. Getting there would require moving through a maze of corridors on the lower decks, where alternate exit routes were virtually nonexistent, getting lost was a real possibility even with the schematics, and there would likely be hundreds of maintenance drones wandering around. And I likely still had at least one other person unaccounted for onboard. Whether they were a crew member, a pirate, or an unusually quick scavenger, I didn't know.

Or a hallucination, I thought dourly.

The fact that they had ignored my hails lent me to the conclusion that they weren't up to anything good. Any reasonable crewman who had been here on a mostly dead ship for a week should have been ecstatic at the thought of rescue, regardless of what trouble the law might bring.

My initial thought upon seeing the state of the *Alea* was that the crew had most likely abandoned ship in the lifeboat. Then I had seen the sheer number of bloodstains and bullet holes onboard. After seeing what they'd done to the lifeboat and emergency suits. I felt reasonably certain that nobody had gotten off the ship alive. If I hadn't been sure I'd seen someone, I would have assumed they all killed each other off or died in whatever event ripped *Alea* apart. But they hadn't. There was one person left. They knew what had happened, they could fill in the gaps in what the flight recorder would know. I looked one more time at the empty slot for the black box and marched off the bridge

Chapter Six

The upshot to what I was doing was that I could get most of the way to Engineering by taking the main lift tube down from the bridge deck. There was a lift to get directly there on the port side, but using it would require me to navigate a maze of jagged metal, most of which was in hard vacuum, and there was nobody to haul me back if I drifted out into the black. As long as nobody dropped the lift on me halfway down, it would be a fairly quick trip from the lowest level of the shaft to *Alea's* single enormous engineering bay. From there I would have to take the maintenance tunnels to the actual archive itself. I had seen the single bay engineering section before on some ships. It posed problems for life support due to the huge volume of space that had to be pressurized, and problems for crew safety because of the lack of compartmentalized vacuum integrity. The only real benefit was that initial manufacturing, and later overhauls, were far cheaper when all the core systems of the ship were localized. You could build in an access point that would allow all major machines to be pulled out and replaced at once, without chasing multiple systems all over the ship. Almost like building a ship in a bottle. You can guess which benefit most big shipping conglomerates tended to care about most. In fairness to *Alea's* shipwrights, they had positioned the access for engineering within the massive cargo bay itself, meaning it was still relatively safe for workers as the cargo bay would act as a sort of dry dock for any major engineering projects. The hatch itself would be a massive, semi-permanent bulkhead of thick metal separating the vacuum of the hold from the pressurized crew compartments.

With the ship's main power down most of the machine would have warmed to somewhere in the mid two-hundreds of the kelvin scale as life support tried to keep the vessel livable. That would kill the computer's ability to process—and its working memory. But unless someone had replaced a two trillion dollar piece of hardware without the owners' knowledge (unlikely), then the flight recorder copy would have been saved to a non-volatile memory medium; i.e. a second identical flight recorder buried in the bowels of the computer. This copy was actually made for me specifically. Or someone like me anyway. It existed so that in the absence of the crew and in the event of the destruction of the bridge, the company could still retrieve a record. It also had the added benefit of being nearly impossible to tamper with, so the company could discreetly check the version of the story they got from any survivors with the mainframe copy if they found the ship's remains. In reality, that was the true black box for the ship, not the remote copy on the bridge.

It wasn't a long trip to the main lift tube from the bridge. If the main airlock hadn't been destroyed in the wreck, I would have passed it already. It wasn't a long trip, but something had changed aboard *Alea*. If before it had felt like there was something else here, now it felt like it was staring at me. Watching every step lead me further down this rabbit hole. After fifty meters I drew my pistol. I've used a lot of weapons over the years, but Jericho's the only one I really trust. Whatever it lacked in ammo or modern amenities, it more than made up for by simply *always working*. That was an invaluable asset to me.

I could have sworn I heard more scuttling as soon as I drew the gun. It would take something a lot bigger than a rogue maintenance bot to take a hit from Jericho and keep kicking. I passed more missing panels, more cut away doors. My lamp blazed through the darkness like a searchlight looking for an escaped convict, cutting left and right as I checked corners, compartments, and gaps in the paneling for frisky drones. By the time the lift doors were in sight, it was getting hard to control my breathing. It felt like there was something huge barreling down the passageway behind me. The clicking was definitely back, louder than ever. I planted my back on a solid section of bulkhead next to the lift doors and swung Jericho up, tracking back and forth between empty hatchways, searching for a target. Nothing. Empty passageways and dead silence. Everything had stopped. I stayed there for a moment, nerves taught. That feeling drudged up some bad memories. I stopped until I got my breathing into a familiar rhythm: four second inhale, four second pause, four second exhale, four second pause, repeat. I imagined lighting a candle and told myself I only had to be calm until the candle burned out. It was an old trick of mine to pack away unhelpful emotions for a while. It took a minute, but the panic subsided to a manageable level, and I narrowed my focus down to the job. The simple job. Go down. Get the record. Get some *answers*. Bug out. I nodded to myself.

Just another job, James...

I almost believed that as I pried the doors to the lift open.

The thing about cosmo-haulers is that they're big. Very, very big. And when you're dealing with big, simple and easy are not synonymous. It was simple to take the lift shaft down. But given that I was essentially solo rappelling a thousand-meter cave shaft to get to the bottom of the ship and Engineering, it wasn't necessarily easy. I would have to descend until I reached the limit of my magnetic grapple, then detach it, reel it down, and reset it before doing another stretch. The real bitch of it was that there was a cargo elevator that went straight to Engineering. But it was a couple hundred meters aft, almost directly across from the *Erebus*, and I had no reason to think that one would work either given the state of *Alea*. And getting there would mean doing a solo EVA on an unstable wreck. The most likely outcome was that I would waste a lot of time picking my way back, only to have to do this process anyway. I could always check if it worked once I got to Engineering, and if it did, I'd save some time on the return trip. I weighed the options as I shone my high-intensity lamp into the shaft. It looked as bad as the rest of the ship. Cannibalized and corroded. The lift rails were twisted and mangled almost beyond recognition.

No chance of a ride back up here then...

I engaged my mag boots and leaned into the shaft, peering up. There were only a couple decks above me, but I couldn't tell if the lift car was jammed up there or not. I held my arm out in the shaft briefly, then relaxed the limb. It fell to my side at a sedate pace.

Call it point two, point three g?

That felt right. It was fairly common to lower the gravity in lift shafts or anywhere you really had to move mass. It was mostly there as a convenience anyway. Working in zero g is always a pain and a little gravity helps avoid the hassle. No reason for a lift to be full Earth standard though, that would just waste energy. Gravity in the shaft wasn't really ideal. If gravity was offline in the lift shaft, I could just walk down the side of the tube like it was another banged up passageway. Gravity meant I would have to descend and potentially deal with fluctuations and debris, and there was of course the risk of free falling a thousand meters down a jagged metal pipe to consider.

I gave the tunnel another look up and down. It looked unsettlingly like an open mouth waiting for prey dumb enough to wander inside. I exhaled through my nose, slowly, then pulled my magnetic grapple from my belt and gave it a quick check. The grapple is a spacer's best friend and always accompanies his suit. Magnetic grapples are meant for one thing above all else: To let you reconnect to your ship during a spacewalk or loss of gravity. They're the last thing standing between you and floating into the abyss if your mag boots fail you, and they've saved a lot of people from being lost in the dark. It's near impossible to find one person in the void if they drift more than a couple hundred meters from the ship. Recovery is much more difficult, much less likely, than most people realize. Believe me; I know from experience. I checked the simple, round electromagnet that served as the head, then eyed the hatch to find the most solid beam available. I picked a good candidate, secured the magnet, and gave it a couple of test pulls, dropping into a sitting position over the deck to check for any give in the anchor.

Solid. Good.

Satisfied that my anchor was secure, I backed up to the hatch, double-checked Jericho and the a-knife in their respective places to make sure they weren't going anywhere, and kicked off the edge.

The tube was a surreal place. Looking down as I kicked out from the wall and sped downward, there was a sense of descending not into the lower decks of a modern-era cosmo-hauler, but into the bowels of an ancient ruin, something that was long forgotten—and better off that way. I still couldn't fathom the state of the ship. I looked around more closely at my first stop, after I had locked my mag boots to a ledge. This lack of maintenance hadn't started when the *Alea* went missing; it couldn't have. It was far too pervasive and advanced. The ship was younger than me, but the more I saw of it the more I wondered if the *Alea* was what salvagers call a dead ringer: A salvaged ship given a new transponder and "built" by a shell corporation for the main company.

Interstellar shipping conglomerates got good subsidies and tax breaks in order to incentivize the building of new ships. A dead ringer let them pocket that money for the shareholders while forking over a fraction of the cost of designing and building a new hull. It was illegal, unethical, and not all that uncommon. I checked the records of each ship I was given for the telltale signs of a ringer. *Alea* hadn't raised any flags to me, but there's always a better shyster out there somewhere and I'm not infallible. I shook my head as I reattached my grapple to a reasonably solid-looking beam. I had about two hundred meters of line on the grapple's spool, so I should have about four more legs before I reached Engineering.

As I kicked off from the ledge to start the second leg of the descent, I found myself fixating on the darkness below me. It seemed to stretch out for a moment, becoming an infinite well of shadows as I contemplated the eight hundred meter drop through the darkness if my grapple failed for some reason. I tore my gaze away and shone my lamp up, towards the top of the ship. I found myself keenly aware of the distance of rotted metal above me, and the fact that the lift may still be up there, slowly working its way free. There would be next to nothing I could do if something came at me after I had kicked off the wall of the lift shaft. Until my boots hit again, I had virtually no ability to control my movement. I shook my head a bit.

The hell is going on with me today?

I felt like a rookie, not someone who had been doing this for the better part of twenty years. While no job is really routine, I wasn't in the habit of jumping at noises or getting into pointless anxiety games about what-ifs on a wreck. I flicked my lamp around, pulling myself into the moment again. Marked wrecks always had a bad aura about them. The kind of feeling you get when you're alone at home and you hear a *bang* downstairs. Or when you're alone in a place usually filled with people. It's a slightly surreal, irrational feeling that you need to keep checking over your shoulder. On *Alea*, it was strong enough to be truly distracting. More than once I thought I saw movement out of the corner of my eye, only to see nothing but the ill-maintained innards of the ship when I looked directly at the spot.

I completed the second leg, then the third and fourth, in eerie stillness. Every time I passed the doorway to one of the decks my skin crawled though. Every one of them looked like it had been busted open. Many had faint streaks of blood around them. There were more along the sides of the shaft. Some part of me constantly expected something to lunge out of the darkness of each new hallway. Shining my lamp down the passageways showed even more advanced disrepair. In some of them the decks and bulkheads themselves seemed warped and bent, like someone had crammed a power loader through them.

I had just started the fifth and final leg of the journey when the paranoia seized me again. After a hundred meters of nothing happening though, even my paranoid senses were starting to relax and consider that maybe this would be a simple job. No sooner had I had that thought than someone grabbed the whole ship and shook it violently. At least that's what it felt like. There was an ear-rending scream of tortured metal and I slammed against one side of the shaft, then the other, then a third. Then I was weightless, tumbling down the tube like a pebble dropped down a gutter, slamming end over end into the bulkheads in a completely uncontrolled descent. The last coherent thought I had was that my body was saying something like I told you so, then an impact and darkness.

...

The vessel was a small platinum miner called *Maneki-neko*. It was from out of system. There weren't many independent miners in Bellerophon space. The *Maneki-neko* was still in unpowered drift when we reached it. There was no visible damage. Crew of thirty-four according to the registry. It was always spooky seeing a ship drifting like that. Something like that, we never knew what we were going to find. They didn't respond to a tight beam hail as we approached. There was a certain amount of tension as we waited for our pilot, Norm Cook, to dock us up. There was a gentle shudder as we made contact, then a series of muffled *thunks* as our locks grabbed onto their airlock, then a high-pitched whine as Norm pressurized the brow. a second later he came over the comms:

"Clamps are good and the brow is pressurized, boys. Might want to check the reactor first, I'm seeing some weird signatures in there. Might explain why their comms are down."

Cobb pulled the lever for the airlock as he replied.

"Roger that Norm, we'll check it out."

The airlock spun open and we crossed into the brow, a temporary tunnel connecting the two ships. *Maneki-neko's* hatch was scuffed and dinged, but in good repair. Cobb activated their airlock.

"You broadcasting the boarding warning, Norm?" He said as the other airlock checked pressures and equalized.

"Yeah. No response, Artie. This one don't look too good from up here."

Cobb grunted.

The airlock finished its cycle and *Maneki-neko's* hatch whooshed open. We crossed into a ready room on the distressed vessel. My suit made every footfall land like a ton of bricks. Ceecee wasn't built for stealth. The ready room contained a few benches, and several lockers of vacuum suits. Everything was brushed with the washed-out light of cheap diodes. One bulkhead held exoskeletons similar to my own, but equipped for mining in the vacuum of the asteroid belt instead of emergency repair tools. The space was dark, but everything seemed to be in order. Wilkins, our engineer, moved to a terminal panel on the wall while the rest of us spread out through the compartment, checking for injured crew or signs of damage. After a moment Wilkins started relaying information to the rest of us.

"Log shows the SOS, then... Holy shit." He stopped talking as we all perked up.

"Care to share with the class, Wilkins?" Cobb prompted. There was a pause.

"Yeah. Yeah. Of course. I just can't... These guys ran a Hail Mary dive." Wilkins' voice was incredulous. I gave a low whistle. "Hail Mary" was a term used to describe a desperate jump made after disabling the safeguards on a ship's reactor, its sub-drive, or both. It was the kind of thing you heard about in barroom stories and nowhere else. Those safeguards were there for a reason. The odds of manually calibrating a reactor or plotting a subspace dive were pretty well described by the phrase "technically non-zero".

"Fuckin' a..." Sinclair said, which I thought summed it up pretty well. Cobb stuck to the job.

"That explains the readings Norm was getting."

"Yeah," Wilkins agreed. "It's a miracle they made it anywhere though."

I moved to inspect the door leading deeper into the *Maneki-neko*. It was locked, which wasn't unusual. Plenty of ships restricted access to spaces that could depressurize the vessel, for obvious reasons.

"I thought that they made it pretty much impossible to circumvent those safeties, Chuck?" I asked Wilkins absently.

There was a pause and I knew he was shaking his head.

"Not if you know anything about what you're doing and you set it up beforehand. Pretty much every engineer puts a backdoor in the operating system for it. Just in case, you know?" Cobb caught that and entered the conversation.

"But not *our* engineer, right Chuck?" He said in a pointed tone.

"...If I say no, will you feel better?"

"Chuck..." Cobb started in a dangerous tone, but Wilkins cut him off.

"Hey, wouldn't you know it, looks like we got an atmosphere leak on the starboard side of the cargo hold. Why don't Harper and I go take care of that?"

Cobb sighed. "Harper can handle the hold. You go get that reactor back on the level. You know the drill, no heroics, stay in touch. Anybody finds crew, you call it in and we get them back to the shuttle for treatment."

That was the unofficial signal that we needed to lock it up and turn to.

"Aye, RT-One," we all chorused. Wilkins unlocked the doors and sent us all the map of the ship he'd cloned from the terminal, and we all filed out to see to our individual tasks. Up until then, it was just another routine day on the job. It's just too bad it didn't stay that way.

...

I came to what could have been fifteen minutes or fifteen hours later, staring crookedly at one of the bulkheads. I was twisted up like a discarded toy, but everything still seemed to be mostly attached correctly. I hurt all over, and my left ankle throbbed unpleasantly, but I was alive. I painstakingly rolled over onto my back and stared up the tube. That fall should have killed me. My suit was designed to match my joints' range of motion perfectly, and the colloid layer would distribute any impacts across almost the whole area of the suit, but that fall must have been almost a hundred meters. In standard gravity it would probably have killed me, suit or no suit. It wasn't until I tried to sit up and felt a jerk that I realized my anchor line hadn't snapped. The beam it was anchored to must have given way. I was lucky I hadn't been killed, or worse, left paralyzed on a derelict. That thought was... unpleasant. I couldn't figure it out. The grapple could have torn free and locked onto something else as I fell. That would have broken my fall somewhat, but it didn't account for the initial impact I had felt. There certainly hadn't been anything big enough to cause that in *Alea's* path when I boarded. And there was the fact that I knew, beyond the shadow of a doubt, that the beam I'd used to anchor my wire was rock solid.

Which could mean it had been destroyed by that impact, or it could mean the beam had been cut. Either by my mystery passenger or by a drone, I couldn't know. One way or the other, my situation had just gotten considerably worse. I cursed, then reprimanded myself.

You knew the risks, James. Bitching won't accomplish anything.

True, I conceded to myself.

I nodded, got my breathing in rhythm, and took stock. My helmet lamp was busted, and the impact had activated the crimson chemical backup next to it. Depending on how long I'd been out, that left me with probably less than twelve hours of good light. The reaction in the chem lamp would continue after that, but the light wouldn't be bright enough to be of much use beyond that point. Forearm computer, trashed. Satchel was still there. I still had Jericho, my knife, and half a spool of fry-wire.

The ammo was missing from my ammo belt, leaving me with only the six rounds already loaded into Jericho.

I nodded to myself. It wasn't the worst set of tools I'd ever had for a problem like this. Well. It might have been. But there was no reason to get whiny about it. I pulled on my grapple, but it was no use. It had become lodged in the debris pile somewhere. It hurt to do it, but I spun open the a-knife and cut the diamond-hard cord at the belt. Then I stood up, and my left ankle screamed at me. Something wasn't right there. I tried a test step, and it barely held my weight. It seethed like a small pocket of molten iron was stuck in the joint. I could move, but only slowly.

Fuck.

No time for whining. My light wouldn't last forever. I tightened my boot straps as far as they would go, then really took stock of my immediate surroundings for the first time. I had come to rest—no, I had slammed into a pile of detritus at the base of the tube shaft, as evidenced by the IXX DECK stenciled on the bulkhead nearby: deck nineteen, the bottom of the boat. The wreckage could have been the remains of the lift car, but I couldn't be sure. The twisted metal blocked two thirds of the doorway, but the was enough room for me to work. I slammed my crowbar into the gap between the doors, hoping the locks hadn't engaged and I could force them apart. If not, I'd have to use up some of my limited fry-wire cutting a hole through the door. I worked the crowbar for a second, but something felt off. There was no give at all. Even when this style of door was locked, you could usually feel at least a little play in the mechanism. I took a closer look in the crimson light of my chem lamp. It was hard to be sure, but... There. Around the edges of the door, the metal had an odd sheen to it, something that looked almost oily. The color steel gets when it's heated past its temper. Say, during welding.

Son of a bitch.

I couldn't be sure, but it looked like the bridge and crew decks hadn't been the only levels to get fortified. I thought for a moment, but I was really out of options. I needed to get through that door to do my job, so it was going to happen. I ran out a quick sketch of a hatch in fry-wire and lit it off. Time was wasting.

The fry-wire was about two thirds of the way through the metal, at a guess, when something at the edge of my hearing registered with my conscious brain. At first, I thought it was just another set of small impacts, but after a few seconds, I realized that it was too regular. It was an odd noise. Almost a patter like rain, then a thump like someone dropping a piece of furniture. Patter, thump. Patter, thump. Patter, thump. It was coming from somewhere above me. Not too far, probably just a couple decks higher than I was, maybe sixteen or fifteen. And it was getting louder.

Shit.

Rattle, THUMP.

I drew Jericho and checked the action.

Rattle, THUMP.

I checked the fry-wire. Almost there.

Come on, burn faster...

Rattle, thump. BANG. Whatever it was, it was at the door to the lift tube. Not on deck fifteen or sixteen. Deck seventeen. Barely more than a dozen feet above me. My gaze flicked back and forth between the molten circle of the wire and the door above me. BANG. The door above me buckled inward six inches. I kicked the center of my circle with my good leg and nearly broke that ankle too. I'd laid out the fry-wire for a standard door, not whatever it had been modified to. I had no way of knowing how much additional metal had been added. I thought for a second, then I snatched Jericho out of the holster and thumbed back the hammer. I only had one idea here. I had no way of knowing if it would work. BANG. The door above me caved another few inches. The wire burned a little deeper. I steadied my breathing. In. Hold. BANG. Out. Hold. I flicked my eyes up to the door above. I couldn't see what tearing the door down, the angle was wrong. One more hit. It would take one more hit. BANG. I had the timing down. In. Hold.

Now!

The BANG from above melded with Jericho's thunderclap. The pistol kicked like a mule as it accelerated a small chunk of tungsten through the compromised door above at a ludicrous velocity. I moved at what felt like a snail's pace. I took a running start and leapt, landing with both feet on the circle of metal the fry-wire had punched out. The impact jarred my ankle terribly, but it gave and I slide through the new hatch. I landed with a grunt on the other side. I only fell two meters or so down to the deck. I slammed on my back hard enough to knock the wind out of me, but not hard enough for the colloid layer in my suit to fully harden. A rockslide of metal and plastoid detritus crashed over me, half burying me. One of the pieces slammed me in the head and knocked me for a loop, but I managed to haul myself upright before stumbling on my bad ankle and slamming into the bulkhead shoulder first. I paused there for a second, trying to gather my thoughts. I took a breath, letting the tension fall for a moment. Which meant that I just about jumped out of my skin when something slammed against the other side of the reinforced door with a thunderous BANG.

There's no fucking way...

I drew Jericho and cocked the hammer. I couldn't see what was on the other side of the hole I'd made--it was plugged with debris from the lift shit, and the impact had only jammed it tighter. But the beauty of Jericho was that I didn't need to be able to see. I lined up a shot and waited for a moment. BANG. As soon as I heard it I pulled the trigger. Jericho roared, and anything in that lift shaft got turned to either slag, or carbon stains. I holstered the trusty weapon with a nod of satisfaction, and limped down the corridor, towards engineering. I made it maybe ten meters before--

BANG.

Fuck this.

Anything that could take two hits from Jericho and keep coming was one seriously tough customer. I wasn't sticking around to try a third shot. I lurched into the best run I could manage, moving by the crimson light of my chemical lantern. The bloody light was sinister, and it seemed to make every shadow flicker and deepen, so that I couldn't tell what might be a vent and what was just the shadow of one of the innumerable pipes and junction boxes covering the bulkheads down here. BANG. Another stumble. I staggered on, but I couldn't see any connecting passages or likely escape routes. I cursed inside my helmet.

Wait.

Up ahead, I saw shadows on either side of the corridor: an intersection! I shambled faster. The banging continued behind me. I could hear the metal starting to tear as the monster made headway against the reinforcement. I made it to the intersection and started to turn left on the simple basis that I was on the leftish side of the passageway when something caught my right arm and almost jerked me off my feet. I struck out with Jericho, still clenched in my fist, and my arm was free. I spun to my right and froze for a second. A bedraggled old man, with hair and beard down to his waist was sprawled on the deck with his hands raised. Another BANG startled us both out of our stare down. the old man's eyes flicked to his left, back the way I had come, then settled back on Jericho. He licked chapped lips and spoke:

"You can shoot me if you like, but if you don't want that thing to get you..."

He stood. Or stooped anyway, and locked eyes with me again.

"Then you'd better follow me as fast as that gimp leg of yours can move."

I held my pistol on him for a second that seemed to stretch, but the banging was still rolling down the corridor towards us, so I lowered Jericho a fraction and nodded.

"Lead on, crewman." He searched my faceplate briefly, but the opaque surface made one hell of a poker face, so he nodded and scrambled to his feet. He jerked the sleeves of his crew jumpsuit nervously, then twitched his head over his shoulder. "This way. I won't hang back if you can't keep up."

Chapter Seven

We scrambled back down the corridor, the old man jogging and me limping furiously. Shadows ebbed and flowed confusingly in the red light of my chem lamp. We twisted through another maze of intersections, making turns that would have seemed almost random if I hadn't noticed my guide running with one hand along the wall and muttering directions to himself under his breath. Not long after our second turn we heard the scream of the lift door finally giving in, and the other man's head whipped around for a moment. Then he shook himself and pushed up his pace. I agreed with the sentiment, but even my fastest limp couldn't keep up. He pulled one meter ahead, then two, and I started to hear that distinctive Patter, Thump from behind me, much faster than when the creature had been coming to investigate the lift shaft. The crewman ducked around a corner ahead of me, at least five meters ahead of me now. I spun around the same corner and saw nothing. Just an empty length of corridor. I scanned the passageway for any sign of my guide, but there was no trace of him. True to his word, he'd left me behind. My gaze raked the passageway furiously, looking for a sign. Something caught my eye, a gap between two of the bulkhead panels. Improvising patches and fixes had been my job in the Patrol; I could recognize an improvised fit when I saw one.

The rattle-thump was getting closer. Not right around the next bend closer, but closer, and fast. I slid my hands around the edges of the panel. It definitely stood out from the bulkhead more than it should, but it didn't yield to a solid pull. I ran my fingers around again and this time my left hand caught on something. I pressed on the small projection one way, then the other. That did it. There was a click, and the hatch popped outward slightly. By this point I could feel the thumps through the soles of my boots. I ripped the panel open and ducked through. I pulled it shut behind me firmly, making sure to hear the snick of the mechanism engaging again. I turned around and found a cramped little tunnel, likely an old duct or run of conduit. It was small enough that I had to crouch awkwardly and my elbows were prone to banging either side of it while I crawled. Given the apparent size of whatever was out there, that seemed like an advantage more than anything. I scrambled as quietly as I could down the passage, fumbling around the awkward twists and turns of the duct as it wound its way through the innards of the ship.

It seemed to change levels almost at random, angling first up, then steeply down and left, then turning right and leveling out. I wasn't nearly as quiet as I would have liked, what with dragging my bum ankle around the turns and keeping Jericho facing forward in case my erstwhile guide had any nasty ideas in his head. I might have been suspecting an innocent victim of a terrible tragedy. Then again, someone had destroyed the e-suits by the bridge, and it didn't seem like the fellow's cup was running over with moral concern for others. That last bit might have been a tad uncharitable, but it's hard to like a man who leaves you to the tender mercies of something than can pound its way through reinforced steel vacuum doors with brute force. The noises from the beast, or machine, or whatever it was, were growing more distant. It didn't seem like it was bashing down the tunnel hatch either, so my heart rate settled into something in the low ultrasonic range.

I had just gotten into a rhythm of crawling that minimized the pain in my leg when I turned a corner and slammed my faceplate directly into something. I cursed to myself and took a look at the offending object. It was a crudely fashioned square of metal, clearly not part of the original design. It sparked a sense of recognition in my mind, and it took me a moment to figure out why. It looked like I had found out where some of that missing metal from the upper decks had gone. It looked like my survivor, most likely one Thom Wilks if his age was any guide, had been putting some of that metal to use down here. I thought of how extensive the cannibalization had been up top. There was no way to know how many of these fortifications had been made throughout the ship.

Industrious fellow...

I slid my hands around the edges of the panel, looking for another one of those crude little spring-latches. Nothing doing. I craned my neck around awkwardly in the cramped space, trying to get the dim red light from my chem lamp into the little nooks and crannies of the space. Some loose wires, a bit of metal sticking out... Wait. I grabbed the little protrusion and gave it a test push in every direction, up, right, down, left. I could have been imagining it, but it felt like there was some play when I pushed it to my left—away from the little hatch. I set my hand and gave it a hearty shove, and after a moment of resistance there was another click. I tested the panel and it pulled out on a crude hinge this time. I scrambled through and yanked it shut. Another click, and I was on my way.

The next quarter-hour was a test of my patience. There were dead ends, false doors, more hidden passages... The place was a labyrinth. It was a staggering amount of work. Some portion of it must have pre-dated the wreck, or the mutiny, whichever came first. I couldn't believe one man could do all this in the two weeks since *Alea* had gone missing. I realized in that time that it wasn't exactly that it was one tunnel that twisted unpredictably: it was one route through a network of tunnels. Dozens of intersections and turn-offs were crudely welded over with the missing panels from up above, pieces of hatches, and whatever else the old coot could get his hands on. I wouldn't have been surprised to see the galley sink in the mix.

Eventually, I came to one hatch that was definitely different from the others. It was better made, less crude. The metal seemed much thicker when I rapped on it. And it had what appeared to be an ancient mechanical lock welded into it. I couldn't get at the bolt as the hatch was too tightly fitted, but there's more than one way to skin a cat. I flicked open my knife and cut the lock out of the crude door in three quick cuts. I punched the cylinder through to the other side with the handles of the knife and drew my pistol. Just in case. I pushed the door open with my left hand, and I was surprised to see a thin bar of light seep through the crack. I gave it a second, then shoved the door wide open and rolled through. I came up to one knee in a compartment. It was moderately sized and dimly lit, but that was all I noticed before someone rushed me. He held a crude

machete over his head in preparation for a strike. I snapped
Jericho on target, one hand bracing the other on the grip just like
I'd always trained.

"Stop! Stop right fucking there!" I barked through my
loudspeaker. He pulled up short, fear crawling over his face. I
stayed that way for a moment to make sure he wasn't about to try
another bum rush, then I spoke.

"Easy, Thom. Just take it easy. Nobody has to get hurt." It
was definitely the same man from the passageway. His age was a
dead giveaway to his identity.

Confusion joined the fear on his face for a moment, as
though I'd said something odd, so I kept going.

"You are Thom Wilks, yes? Senior Engineer's mate?"

The confusion on his face cleared, and he lowered his
improvised weapon. He nodded slowly, then swallowed a couple
of times.

"Yeah... Yeah, I'm Thom Wilks. Haven't heard my own
name in a while though."

He looked over my shoulder at the open hatch.

"Thought you were dead meat."

He glanced back at me.

"No hard feelings, you understand."

I nodded. "No hard feelings," I agreed.

He tugged nervously at his sleeves again, the same tick I'd noticed in the passageway. Then he made and abortive gesture towards the door.

"Do you mind if I..." I nodded an approval, and he skirted around me in a wide berth to get to the door. I kept him in my peripheral vision, but I used his motion to scan the room with a few quick flicks of my eyes. The light was coming from one of those old electrolytic lanterns, the kind you can keep running on any salt water solution, and it cast a cold, blue white half-light over everything. It mixed unpleasantly with the light from my chem lamp. The place could only really be described with terms like *rat hole* and *hovel*. The room was roughly ten meters by fifteen, and I couldn't ascertain its intended use through the clutter. It seemed like old Thom had grabbed everything that might be of use in the future, and plenty of things that were outright useless, and socked them away down here. It seemed like a sizeable number of the missing panels from above were down here, but not nearly enough to account for any major portion of the stripped out upper decks.

Cases of ration packs were stacked around the rooms, and what seemed like hundreds but was probably closer to dozens of empty wrappers littered the floor like some kind of aluminized fungi. There were tools of various descriptions, a very battered old space suit, and a filthy nest of rags that seemed to be Mr. Wilkin's stand-in for a bed. Thom cursed from down in the hole.

86

The rough little door clanked shut and my gaze snapped back to Thom. He was staring back at me with unnerving intensity, as though I was something important written in a language he couldn't read. I was suspicious of the man. Someone had been on the upper decks when I showed up, and it was highly likely my fall down the lift shaft had been sabotage. It could have been another one of the crew, or it could have been Mr. Wilks. I was already injured, fatigued, and in a bad spot. I wasn't really feeling a leap of faith. On the other hand, I had never found another survivor from a marked wreck before. This man might have the answers I'd been looking for. I *needed* to hear what had happened on *Alea*. I watched Thom. he watched me. His eyes flicked to Jericho, and I slowly lowered the gun. Then I holstered it, but I kept my shooting hand on the grip. My consideration has definite limits. Hopefully Thom wasn't in a mood to test them.

"Now that we're both feeling a little more civil, Mister Wilks, we need to sort some things out. My name is James Harper. Why did you run from me on the upper decks? I could have gotten you out of here hours ago."

He twitched again, and I stopped, but it seemed like just another one of his tics, so I kept going:

"I'm a cosmonautical investigator. I was sent out here by the owners of the *Alea* to determine why your ship went dark."

I leaned forward slightly and made good use of my helmet's opaque visor for a little intimidation.

"I need to know what the hell happened here, Thom. Your company only reported you dark two weeks ago. Why does it look like there was a civil war up there? And what the hell was that thing in the elevator shaft?"

Mr. Wilks blinked rapidly for a few seconds and tried to say something, but it just came out as a rough kind of *haah* sound. He licked his lips and tried again.

"That's the big one."

I cocked my head to the side.

"What?"

"In the lift shaft. He's the big one. The biggest one. There are the small ones and the biggest one, and—"

He went into some kind of fit then, twitching back and forth. I had my doubts about old Thom. I wasn't real optimistic about Thom's chances of ever making a full psychological recovery.

"Focus, Thom. The Big One? The big what? What the hell is out there? Bots?"

He shook his head.

"Not xenos, surely?" Xeno-organisms had been hypothesized for centuries, sure, but in all our exploration we'd never found any. I don't consider myself a close-minded person, but I had never seen any sign of non-human intelligent life before. Not on wrecks, marked or otherwise. Not anywhere else. Thom shook his head at xenos though, and he just went back into a twitching fit at any mention of the thing in the lift shaft, so I put a pin in the topic of our big fellow passenger. Over the next half-hour, between his bouts of mute twitching and staring, I managed to piece together his rough account of what had happened.

According to on Thom Wilks, tensions between the crew began mounting after responding to a distress call. midway through here last scheduled voyage. The lower ranking crew, according to him, mutinied against himself and the other senior staff when they found out that the delay from responding to the call would cost them all dearly. In a bid to achieve leverage, the mutineers seized main engineering, cutting it off from bridge control, and reprogrammed a large cargo mech to breach the defenses on the command deck. The flight log had been taken by the captain, who had attempted to escape on the *Alea's* only lifeboat. Wilks said that the remaining officers elected to enter into a voyage without sufficient data, resulting in *Alea* being caught at the terminator between real and subspace, and consequently suffering catastrophic damage.

Wilks claimed that was when he had made an escape to the lower decks through maintenance tunnels and emergency ladders. He claimed not to know what had happened after that. Thom figured he had been alone for at least three months. He had no answers about where the rest of the crew might be or how many had survived, and he refused to believe only two weeks had passed. He made no mention of strange symbols or anything more inexplicable than human greed and frustration.

It did fit what I'd found. Time dilation on crossing the terminator was a known phenomenon; but the nature of a subspace transit meant you crossed that boundary under the protection of a sub-drive, which prevented direct interaction with the terminator. This would be a freakishly unlucky accident if that was the case. But a mutiny would explain the shootout, and the failed transit could explain the state of the ship. But there was more than one problem.

For one thing, where were the rest of the crew? Thom claimed he knew of no other survivors when pressed. He said that he had assumed the failed transit had damaged the ship and sent the various drones and the heavy mech he called the big one out of control, and that they had subsequently killed the rest of the crew. He claimed to know nothing about the massacre on the bridge, having hidden belowdecks before the bridge was sealed shut, but that he had encountered some haywire maintenance drones over the past few months. I turned the story and our circumstances over in my head for a few minutes, and consulted my mental map of the ship.

That led me to two conclusions; one, Thom's story didn't give me the answers I was after. Two, the best way to get answers and get off the *Alea* was to go through the primary engineering space, recover the black box, and then use the cargo lift on the port side of the space to get back to the crew deck and get off of *Alea*. I simply couldn't canvas the entire ship for survivors, especially not with an army of hostile mechanicals roaming the vessel. I turned my helmet to Thom and spoke firmly:

"Alright, Mister Wilks, here is what's going to happen. I need to get to data engineering central and access the secondary copy of the flight recorder. You are going to lead me to Engineering, I'll get the record, and we will use the cargo lift, or failing that, the shaft, to return to my ship and leave this tragedy behind us. None of these things are optional. Do you understand me Mister Wilks?"

Thom flinched when my helmet swiveled to face him directly. Then he licked his lips.

"There's... There's no secondary copy of the flight record. It's all in the one on the bridge. If—if you lost that one..."

He trailed off, shrugging helplessly.

Not much of an engineer...

A competent Engineer would know about the second copy of the log, but then Wilks had been through an ordeal in the past few weeks. I didn't bother to refresh his memory. It was uncharitable but I thought it was also clear from the state of the *Alea* that Thom wasn't a competent Engineer. And besides. There were a lot of clocks ticking down now, for both of us. We needed to move, so I just shook my head and pushed on:

"What I need is there, even if there isn't a full record. We move now, before the situation onboard deteriorates even further. Grab anything you'll need once we get off the *Alea*: we won't be coming back again."

If I had expected the castaway to be excited about the news that his exile was over, I would've been disappointed. He only redoubled the shaking of his head and the wringing of his hands and tried to stammer something out with the hollow shell of his voice. It took him a few tries to articulate what he was trying to say, but he eventually got it out.

"We—we can't go up. Up is where the big one lives. We go up there, it'll get his attention, and he'll come take us too. Down, maybe, Engineering, I can take you there, we can go through the old coolant lines. but not up. I won't go up. It won't let you past."

Honestly, I got where he was coming from. I wasn't at my most mobile, and he was a few ships short of a fleet. We weren't the ideal pair to be fighting an uphill battle. Or an upstairs battle, in our case. But the only way out was through. There was no chance of anyone else coming out to get us, there were no escape pods, and there was no way to communicate with the outside world. So I put my right hand on the butt of Jericho and stared Thom down through my visor in the half-light.

"We go. There are absolutely no other options, you have no way off this wreck without me, and most importantly, I'm under contract to get that information and bring back any survivors. No matter how big that mech is, it can't be in more than one place at once, and I made it through the upper levels just fine on my way down here. So pick up your balls and lead the fucking way, Mister Wilks. I have a contract to honor."

And answers to find, I added silently.

92

It should be said that I'm hired for my proficiency, not my people skills. And Thom did get his ass in gear after that. He stuffed a few random odds and ends into a bag made of a knotted up old blanket and led the way through another concealed hatch. I hadn't noticed it before, and I reminded myself that Mr. Wilks might be more than a little mad after his ordeal, but he certainly wasn't stupid. I didn't particularly like that combination.

Thom led me through another twisting maze of partially blocked off vents and maintenance crawlspaces, winding lower and lower through the belly of the ship. Along the way it occurred to me that there would have been almost no use for the schematics I had brought. Between the routine changes made to a ship throughout the course of its life and the many, many changes old Thom had made, the interior passageways down here bore little to no resemblance to the original plans. There didn't seem to be any real rhyme or reason to the path Thom had secured for himself, but then I didn't know where it was supposed to go.

Thom explained that when the mutineers had seized the engineering section, they had welded everything but the cargo lift shut and reinforced their barricades, so we would be going through the old coolant lines for the sub-drive to get in. According to him, they had still been active when the mutiny occurred, so they couldn't have been reinforced. They were empty now because they had been deliberately vented into engineering, killing all the mutineers within. We would have to cut a new access into the tunnels in order to get into the actual coolant lines, the designers of the ship having failed to account for the needs of injured cosmonautical investigators when they drafted their original plans, but I had enough fry-wire to get us in, I was sure.

After a quarter hour or so of clambering awkwardly through the tunnels behind my newest friend while his mutterings shifted from complaints to dire imprecations and lost a good deal of coherence, we stopped somewhat abruptly in an unremarkable stretch of maintenance crawlspace.

"Here," Thom said shortly.

I glanced around the tunnel.

"You're certain?" I asked. He glanced at me sharply.

"Of course I'm sure. I've spent most of my life on this boat, this section parallels the coolant tunnels the most closely."

I nodded and spooled out some fry-wire, marking out a rough trapezoid shape on the side of the crawlspace he indicated. An artist I am not. I shooed Thom to the far side while the wire did its work. I pointed my helmet at the soon-to-be hatch, but I kept my eyes on old Thom, to see what he would do when he thought I wasn't looking. Either I was paranoid or he was just too smart for that move, because he just muttered to himself the same way he had been doing since we met.

Once the wire completed its circuit, I kicked the new hatch through the hole and motioned Thom to wait while the edges cooled. Then I drew Jericho and slithered through the hole. The only illumination was the crimson glow seeping from my chem lamp, and it made the smooth walls of the coolant tunnel seem uncomfortably like the digestive tract of some giant beast. Wonderful thought. I turned to the hatch and motioned

Thom through, now that I knew we weren't going to be ambushed by a horde of murderous maintenance bots. He slipped through the hole with surprising ease for a man as... Weathered as he was, and gestured down the tunnel to my right.

"That way to the nearest inspection hatch," he said absently.

I motioned for him to lead, and we set off. The inspection hatches were used for the periodic inspection tests of the tunnels, when a certified inspector would come down here to check the state of the tunnels and ensure that they wouldn't do anything undesirable, such as venting all the coolant into the engineering space and killing everyone inside. It wouldn't surprise me to learn that the *Alea's* owners hadn't had these tunnels inspected in decades. Ship owners were notorious for cutting costs on maintenance and inspections to save an easy buck. After all, those cost a good deal of money, even if the inspector didn't find anything. And God forbid they did find a problem, which the owners would then be legally required to fix.

No, better to just let sleeping dogs lie and keep some money in the investors' pockets. After all, it wasn't their lives on the line if these systems failed. At any rate, it didn't take long before we spotted the inset rungs running up the side of the tunnel that indicated a service hatch. Thom clambered up to spin the wheel of the hatch, the sleeves of his too-small jumpsuit pulling up his skinny, arms as he strained ineffectually. A bruise peeked out from under one sleeve. Life was rough on the *Alea*. Something about that caught in my mind, and my wheels started turning. He gave it a few tries before he stopped, panting, and clambered down the ladder. I took his place and forced the seized wheel to spin with moderate difficulty.

I heaved with one arm and threw the hatch up and over, wincing slightly as it clanged thunderously on the deck. I drew Jericho and climbed the rest of the way of the ladder one-handed, sweeping the compartment as soon as I had my boots on solid metal. The space was odd. It was absolutely cavernous, as evidenced by the overhead looming above like a bank of storm clouds, but the deck was cluttered with gargantuan pieces of machinery and meter wide runs of conduit and pipe. I scanned the multitudinous points of concealment with the kind of amusement you can only muster when life throws you three or four curveballs all at once. If there was ever a place and time that was perfect for an ambush, this was it. I circled around the hatch deliberately so I was behind Thom when he climbed through, and made sure he heard me cock Jericho's hammer. I aimed the hand cannon at the center of his back and said two words with all the force of command I could muster, and a former boarding team leader can muster quite a bit.

"Isacc Bly!"

The old man flinched and turned reflexively. He caught himself quickly, but it was enough. Enough to confirm what I had seen when he went up the ladder the first time. That thing that had caught in my brain had come to me when I was clearing the room. An entry from the registry I had reviewed before coming onboard. *Name: Isacc Bly. Age: 17. Distinguishing characteristics: tattoo on left forearm, subject blue koi fish.* I looked at the wizened old man in front of me. *Age: 17.*

96

Gods above.

Chapter Eight

'Thom Wilks", real name Isaac Bly, slowly turned to look into the visor of my helmet. I looked into his eyes through the shaded composite and I saw the truth of the man there, just how broken he really was.

"That's you, isn't it?" I asked quietly.

He swallowed, then nodded. He was beginning to cry.

"Yes..." His voice broke. "Yes, it is."

I closed my eyes, just for a second.

Hells bells and buckets of blood...

When I opened them, I asked another question whose answer I didn't want to have to live with. It was just the latest in a long line.

"How long, Isaac?"

He laughed once, and there was a hysterical edge to it. He wasn't tugging on his sleeves or muttering anymore. He was calm. Dead calm.

"How long... You're going to find, Mister Harper, that *time* is a meaningless word on this ship. Time doesn't mean much when you have no way to tell the minutes or hours apart, when you get so used to the smell of offal that you forget what clean air smells like. I don't even know who Isaac Bly was anymore. Isaac Bly didn't survive the mutiny, much less the hell that came after. Isaac Bly couldn't have done what he needed to do to survive."

My stomach sank down to sit on the deck plates. I had heard other men and women talk like this. I still had bad dreams about what they described doing. And what I had to do after. I steadied Jericho and drew a breath in through my nose. Let it flow out through my mouth.

"What did you do, Isaac?" He quirked a little half-smile at me. Hysteria glimmered in his eyes.

"Only what I had to, James. See I won't wind up like the others. Twisted into—" he broke off and horror crawled across his features like a spider.

"—Into *things*. That was the deal, you see. I give them the others, plus one, and when it's done I get to die a real death. Not what happened to old Thom and them, caught between like this damned ship. But you..."

His eyes roved over me hungrily. "You're the last one I need, James Harper. They want you very, very badly, my friend.

Badly enough to damn me and my whole crew to hell just to get you here."

I don't consider myself a skittish man or a coward, but that I did not like. I felt my features harden.

"Who wants me here, Isaac? And what do you mean, they damned you to get me here?" He smirked in that nasty way again.

"You don't get it, do you James? All of this," He waved around at the cavernous bay, indicating the entire ship with the gesture.

"*All* of this, was because of you. You think they're stupid? You think they didn't notice someone going around spitting in their eye? Covering up their handiwork? Sending all their little gifts into the void? Of course they noticed. And they do not like it."

His expression became almost smug as he warmed up.

"See, I'm smarter than they realize, James, and I've picked up a few things from them over the last few decades of hell. They're planning something, Harper. And whatever you're doing, it's getting in the way. I don't know the specifics, but I know there's a deadline for whatever they're doing, and sending things back from the other side is costly. So they set all this up, and when I offered my services, they gave me a name. Your name. All I had to do was get you here, so you couldn't leave, and then I get to die."

He closed his eyes and a hopeful, peaceful expression crossed his face. Like a man waiting for rain, or maybe a blessing.

"Just once, like a man should."

Still smiling, he moved faster than I would have believed possible, grabbing the lip of the service hatch and slamming it shut. There was a ratcheting series of clicks, and I felt my stomach dip again. The hatch could be opened from the inside as an emergency measure. But it auto-locked on the outside to prevent tampering. I started to hear chittering from all around us, and rattling clicks. Isaac smiled at me and started to speak:

"Just let it happen, Harper. It won't make it better but you'll never--"

We'll never know what I wouldn't do, because I wasted one of my six rounds of ammunition for Jericho blowing Isaac Bly's torso across the deck. The round vaporized most of his torso without noticing it was there and lanced across the room in a line of fire, slamming into a machine the size of a house and blowing a hole the size of a sofa into the solid metal. Isaac was right in the end. He did get to die for bringing me here.

The chittering was getting louder, so I picked the direction where the noise seemed the least loud and started running, every step lancing through my injured ankle like a hot knife. I vaulted over and slid under pipes as the noise rose to a cacophony around me, a constant barrage of sound. Then I started to see them. I had been half right. They were maintenance bots... Or they had been.

They all seemed to have been damaged in some way and then repaired with various human body parts. Ribs and fingers replaced the spider like legs of the maintenance bots, often still covered in gore, some of which was dried out like jerky or rotting, and some of which was still horrifyingly fresh. Each was marked with a luminous glyph somewhere on its hideous body. There were thousands of them. More bots than there should be on the *Alea* and too many body parts for the limited crew. Despite the flagrant illogic of the things, they moved with a terrible agility, leaping from machine to machine easily, swarming towards me. I had a few meters of fry wire, three rounds left in Jericho, and my atomic knife.

Shit. Shit, shit, shit.

I spun around, not panicking—not yet—but scanning furiously for anything that I could use. I wracked my brain for anything useful that I could remember from the schematics. I couldn't think of anything. As the puppets closed in, the lights of their glyphs like a bloody field of stars, all I could think that I was trapped down here in engineering, as far as possible from *Erebus* and escape. My leg snagged on the lip of the service hatch as I turned, and I cursed. Then I froze for a moment.

103

Wait.

It clicked. That was it. I thought of the schematics as I hobbled away from the swiftly approaching horde of horrors. It could work. I could pull this off. I just had to make it. I could see my goal embedded in the aft bulkhead, rising over the huge machines that cluttered the floor. I adjusted my course to the right and sprinted, destroying my ankle more every meter in the hope of keeping the rest of my body alive. I was almost there, but the swarm was only a few meters behind me.

Something hit my back, and I felt it trying to bite through my suit with whatever passed for fangs. It felt like someone slamming a pair of pliers closed on my shoulder blades repeatedly. I grabbed the thing with my left hand and flung it off. I heard it smack into a section of pipe more than saw it, heard the squeal, like a teakettle. Apparently they felt some kind of pain. I drew my a-knife and slashed through conduits and cable as I went, trying to clutter the way. For the first time that day, I had a minor stroke of luck. One of the cables I slashed was live, and it charged the deck and metalwork around it, frying dozens of the nightmarish monsters as they tried to cross the deck zone. Even in my top-of-the-line suit I felt the charge, and I stumbled as my legs spasmed, but it bought me the time I needed.

I made it to the bulkhead I had been aiming for, but I had come off course. I needed to run another twenty meters along the bulkhead to reach the spot I needed. This gave the monsters time to flank me and cut me off, and more flung themselves at me. Individually they might not have been a threat, but as half a dozen tried to gnaw through my suit, I could feel them making headway.

104

Eventually, they would get through. I slashed with my a-knife, but I had to be careful that the sub-molecular edge didn't take off one of my own limbs in my haste. I stumbled forward as more piled onto me and around my knees. I felt them trying to tear though my suit. The suit was warning me of multiple imminent breaches as I fell to my knees short of my goal. I struggled against a dozen of them to draw Jericho and raise it. I couldn't raise my head, there were too many dragging my helmet down. I roared with the effort of raise Jericho, aiming at where I thought the right spot was. Only my right hand and my trusty hand-cannon remained above the mass of the abominations. Something that had been in my head ever since I arrived at this wreck slipped from my lips in a whisper:

"*Alea iacta est...*"

The die is cast. I pulled the trigger.

Chapter Nine

I heard the detonation of Jericho firing, and explosion as the hyper-dense alloy round impacted, and the roar of coolant as one wall of sound beneath the sea of monstrosities. I heard a roar, and then a sound almost like thousands of windows cracking all at once. The attempts to break through my suit vanished, as a torrent of liquid rushed around me and immobilized me. I was frozen, literally, kneeling with one hand on the deck, my head bowed, and my right arm outstretched in the shot that saved my life.

I could barely take shallow breaths because the exterior of my suit was completely frozen over. All sound in the room had stopped, and the sudden temperature change had slowed the reaction in my chem-lamp, dimming it to the barest glow. I knelt there straining to get enough oxygen to recover from my mad dash with too-shallow breaths, listening for the sound of claws on ice that would mean death for me. There was nothing. Nothing but the cracking of frost and frozen oxygen, and occasionally the snap of bone or ceramic succumbing to the cold. The reserve coolant tank I had shot must have had most of its liquid gas coolant still in reserve, which was a minor miracle considering how long *Alea* had been travelling through subspace, crawling with monstrosities.

The coolant had frozen the crawling monstrosities into uselessness, at least for the time being, but they had also formed a cage around me, locking me in the chilly grasp of a hand made from thousands of bones and machined parts. I didn't know if they would resuscitate when they thawed, and I didn't want to know. I took stock. Jericho wouldn't be of further use with this particular problem, and the fry-wire was stuck on my belt where I couldn't get at it. My a-knife would get me out but it was locked into my left hand, which was currently planted on the deck beneath a thin layer of oxygen ice and the legs of several of the drones. Immobile. If I could just get a jump start on the thaw...

But the only heat source I had was my own fading body. Even my suit wouldn't last forever against the chill of near absolute zero coolant, and I could already feel the cold gnawing through the layers of carbon weave and ceramic microplating. I was trying to figure out how long I had before my body temperature hit lethal levels when an idea occurred to me. A bad idea, but given that it was a bad day I was in no position to be picky.

I shifted as much as I could, which is to say hardly at all, but it let me confirm that my left hand was almost directly beneath the chin of my helmet. I took a deep breath, put my lower lip between two of my canines, and cracked my chin against the bottom of my helmet. There was a lance of pain, and then hot blood began to fill my mouth with the taste of salt. I waited a moment for my mouth to fill up, then cracked the seal and spat a glob of blood down. I heard a hiss as the hot liquid evaporated some of the frozen oxygen. I tested my hand; movement, but not much. I spat out more blood, and there was a crack. I jerked, and I had a hand free.

The a-knife carved through the frozen drones with little trouble after that, and after a tense few minutes of using the sharpest tool in the galaxy blind and half-numb, I hauled myself out of the pile of limbs, bones and parts. The engineering space looked strange in the dim light of my chem lamp. Above me, the rear bulkhead was strained from the destruction of the coolant tank. Every surface was covered in frost, lending the place the look of a forgotten colony on some ice world in the far reaches of space. If only. I limped through the towering pieces of machinery, stumbling on my busted ankle the whole way.

If my memory of the layout was correct, I was on the wrong side of the space from the logs after my run from the horde of altered maintenance bots, and I was having a hard time recalling where the nearest route up would be. I was past giving a damn about the flight recorder, but I still needed information: I couldn't leave the *Alea* intact for some poor sap to find later, and I needed some specific information to scuttle the ship. First, I needed the serial number of the reactor.

That would tell me certain things I would need to know in order to scuttle *Alea* and still have enough time to get back to *Erebus*. Second, I needed to find alternate ways to get up to the top deck and get the hell out of dodge. There were two lifts that I knew about, but given the degree of planning that had gone into this trap I was wary of taking such predictable routes. The only thing that would be keeping *Erebus* safe would be the fact that I had picked the airlock I used mostly at random, and Isaac Bly seemed to have been the only semi-reasoning creature onboard the *Alea*. The ship was sealed through reasonably secure means, but whatever the big thing was that had driven me down here, the airlocks on *Erebus* wouldn't hold it for long.

I took a deep breath. My heart rate was spiking into dangerous territory. It's one thing to investigate wrecks alone, knowing that no one would listen to my distress call, or send another crew out even if they did. It was another thing entirely to realize that I had walked into a trap custom made for me, and now I was at the bottom of what amounted to a skyscraper filled with hostiles. And my only slim chance of survival was at the top.

Chapter Ten

I hobbled along the floor of the cavernous, pitch-black engineering space like an insect scuttling through a dark warehouse, dwarfed by the sheer scope of the machinery around me. In the dim light of my shuttered chem lamp, it was like walking through the ruins of a city, like pictures from the Omega War where three was nothing bur carnage and rubble left. The titanic machines that were once the beating heart of *Alea* had almost all been ruined, presumably in the same cataclysm that split the ship. I found myself climbing over gears and chunks of metal the size of skimmers, the guts of what were once marvels of science and engineering. I would have had a hell of time locating the piece of equipment I needed if cosmonauts weren't so fond of spraying labels onto everything in block letters. There were still tools scattered in some places, abandoned when calamity befell the ship, and I even passed a half dozen empty docks for casualty control exoskeletons. I eyed it wistfully as I passed, thinking of what I could do with one of those marvels. A good CC suit turned one man into a whole team when emergency repairs were needed on a ship like this, allowing major work to be done with very few hands and without the need for expensive drones.

If I had one of those bad boys...

If I had one of those, this situation would be very different. I'd be doing a lot less running for sure. But if wishes were fishes, we'd all cast nets, and it had obviously been a long time since the suit had been taken, no doubt broken down and turned into some monstrosity now wandering the passageways of *Alea*, or else lost in some godforsaken corner of the ship. The odds of finding one after all this time were laughable. I couldn't help one last glance though.

What I wouldn't give...

The most unnerving thing about the trip to the processor was the silence. After arranging to get me all the way out here and ambushing me with a horde of monsters, whatever was pulling the strings was far, far too quiet for my liking. I couldn't imagine that was a good thing. There were only so many ways out of this room, and I was giving the other side plenty of time to set up more ambushes on all of them. And I only had one good leg. There were other options, but they all came with their own risks.

The upshot to the situation was the constant flood of endorphins to my body meant that it was a lot easier to ignore my bad ankle, which was a real godsend. It still hurt, but it was easier to push the pain to the side, for the moment. Eventually though, the ankle would reach a point where it couldn't bear weight, and then I would be well and truly fucked. There were no two ways about it: I was in a bad situation. I was alone on a derelict with an unknown number of hostiles between me and my only way off the ship. I was injured, tired, and my air, water, and light were all finite. But there wasn't much to do about any of that but keep moving forward. So I just kept limping forward. I felt shaky, and my stomach roiled. But I had a job to do, and the answers I'd gotten so far had only raised more questions. I didn't know what could create a swarm of...

Cyborgs? Flesh-puppets?

...Whatever they were. I didn't know what could do that, but the answers were there. On *Alea.*

To make everywhere like Alea... I tried to imagine that as I limped through the frozen engineering space. A station or planet, slowly descending into this... Hell. It was a sickening thought. I thought about *Erebus*, waiting patiently for me a kilometer above my head. I could probably get there, get out. Just leave *Alea.* I knew my limits. I paused, leaning against a pipe big enough around that it would take three of me to get my arms around it. I dropped my chin to my chest. If I was honest, I wanted to do just that. It wasn't as though I would tell anyone else that they were obligated to try to take on a ship full of monsters by themselves. It was suicide, in all likelihood. There was no way to clear something like *Alea.* But I thought of running. Of *Alea* reaching somewhere populated with innocent men, women, and children. And I asked myself a simple question:

Will that excuse still let you sleep at night then, James?

No. No it wouldn't. I would know. Nobody else might, but I would know that whatever chance those people had, it had died when I decided to save my own skin. And if I was really honest with myself... I wouldn't really be missed. Ever since... Ever since the mission that sent me searching for answers, I hadn't really

113

been a part of society. I had no real friends, no family left. It wouldn't be much of a loss if I didn't make it out, in the grand scheme of things. But I might have a shot to give a few decent people a chance. And maybe I could really answer my questions, make sense of things finally. I nodded to myself, then pushed of the pipe and limped forward, with more determination if not more grace. My destination was the same: my only chance of stopping the *Alea* from doing whatever it was supposed to do was to scuttle the ship. I had some ideas about that, but I would still need to get to the processor. I needed information.

Chapter Eleven

By the time I found my way to main processor on the starboard side of the main engineering space my ankle had become impossible to ignore. I had entered on the port side of the space, then run to the aft bulkhead trying to get away from the swarm, then had to make my way forward and to starboard to get to the immense computer, and the leg was starting to get worse. I found myself casting wary glances at the overhead of the cavernous bay, trying to figure my odds of making it all the way up to the top side of the ship before something found me that I couldn't beat with a cheap trick. I was under no delusions about the last ambush; sure, I'd done some quick thinking, but the only reason I was still alive was because I was lucky, and I knew it. if the coolant had leaked out of that tank, I would've died. If the swarm hadn't clustered so tightly, I would've died. If my suit had failed at any point, I would've died. So now I needed to be smart. I needed information, and there was a way to get it, if whatever had set up this trap didn't know about it.

The set of data stored in the black box of any cosmo-hauler is extensive. Its purpose is to assist in the forensic reconstruction of a crash and account for all personnel and cargo onboard the ship at the time of the crash. It includes schematics, lading, navigation logs, and personnel records, all imprinted onto a carbon microfilm roll and packaged in a carbon matrix and ceramic cassette, in order to make sure it survives as much as possible. I needed two specific sets of information from the computer: The image of the reactor's control OS, and schematics detailed enough to tell me whether I had any other options for getting back to the *Erebus* other than the personnel and cargo lifts.

I wouldn't bring any copy back to an inhabited system for any price. Before I had believed it could be dangerous; now I knew I was stuck onboard a targeted weapon of mass destruction, and I had to treat everything on it as a contamination risk. Possibly even myself. But I'd fucked up and lost my only set of plans in the fall, and I needed this. So I found myself lobotomizing *Alea's* brain like some kind of demented scavenger, working as quickly and quietly as I could to get to the backup record.

It was meant to be recovered by a full salvage team, and was only checked during a full tear-down of the ship's main processor, which meant that I was going to have to do something I didn't want to. Ordinarily the entire assembly would be pulled apart by derricks and crews and bots would have free access to the entire processing and data bank, the whole building-sized computer on display, and usually in zero-g. If you weren't in dry dock, the minor maintenance was meant to be handled by service drones.

What that meant for me was that in order to get the information I needed I was going to have to crawl through ducts meant for service drones, find the correct cartridge, and get back out. I found myself staring into the inky maw of a shaft that was never meant to accommodate an actual human. My breath was a little shaky and so were my hands. So I pictured my imaginary candle, told myself another lie about being calm, pulled Jericho and the A-knife from their holsters, and climbed into the mouth of the abyss. Someone once told me that in one of the wars back on earth some guys used to have to do this kind of thing all the time. Tunnel Rats, he said they were called. The name seemed apt. Time to take a trip into a claustrophobe's idea of hell.

The shaft was just barely big enough for me to crawl awkwardly, dragging my bad leg behind me and slamming my damaged ribs into the sides of the shaft with painful regularity. I didn't have schematics for this particular computer, but I had enough experience to have a good guess on where the record would be. It was meant to be the last remaining part of the ship's computer in the event of a crash, so it would be in the deepest, most protected set of racks, in the very center of the machine. Of course. I had been out-thought on multiple levels here, and that scared me as much as anything.

Whoever or whatever was calling the shots here, they knew me well enough to know that I would pursue the black box backup, out of arrogance and curiosity. I needed enough information to give me an edge. So I hauled my busted body through the crawlway with as much alacrity as I could manage, twitching at every intersection and craning my neck to throw sharp glances behind me. At what I figured was roughly the halfway point, something changed. I couldn't put my finger on what, but something else had arrived. I couldn't feel the rattle-THUMP I'd heard earlier, but that didn't by any means put me in the clear. The enemy had clearly shown an ability to make plenty of smaller foot soldiers to get things done, and there were no coolant tanks to save me in here. If they flooded the tunnels with those little monsters from earlier...

I crawled faster, dragging my body through the turns. The exhaustion was starting to show through. I wasn't quite as quick. Not quite as sharp as I should have been. As I needed to be. The sense of malevolence was getting stronger, and every now and then I thought I caught a slithering, sliding sound coming from behind me. It was getting closer. I hit one dead end, had to back track, then nearly took a tunnel I'd already checked. Then, down a tunnel to my right, I saw it. The tunnel had been partially crushed, but I could clearly make out a maintenance hatch with the words

DATA STORAGE: KEEP SEALED

stenciled on it in black paint.

I nearly sobbed with relief. I scrambled down the tunnel, smashing my torso flat to get through the caved in portion. The tunnel had been flattened down like a box someone stomped on, and I couldn't take a full breath in the narrow confines. Any attempt to do so resulted in a panic-inducing sensation of being restrained, of a giant hand closing around my torso and squeezing the oxygen out. I focused on the image of that blue candle for the fear, reminding myself I only had to be in control until the candle went out, and I kept myself going. I had to turn my head sideways to fit into the smashed tunnel, so I couldn't look ahead or behind me. I was forced to stare at the wall of the tunnel and try not to breathe heavily enough to get stuck or panic. One step at a time.

Reach. Drag. Reset. Reach. Drag. Reset. Reach. Drag—I didn't move forward. I shifted, and managed to huff out a weak

"No,"

as I realized what I had failed to account for. The collapsed portion of the tunnel wasn't uniform. I was stuck. I tried to shove myself back, then I tried to wriggle to the sides. No luck. I slumped for a second, breathing too heavily and feeling the tunnel push back against my ribcage every time.

That was when I heard something slither into the tunnel behind me. It was a wet, slippery sound, like a pile of heavy rope sliding into a puddle. The flame on my candle flickered, and I struggled to heave myself forward. My gloves slipped on the deck, then caught, and I felt myself start to slip forward, through the too-small gap. I huffed out all the air in my lungs, trying to be as small as possible. If I could just get to the other side, I could at least turn around and see what was behind me. I was still stuck staring at the dingy side of the maintenance corridor, immobile and for all intents and purposes blind. I heaved again, and I made a little more progress.

I reset my hands and strained... and something wrapped around my ankle. I managed to huff out another desperate

"No!"

and then I was ripped out of the sticking spot by my injured leg. My leg lit up with pain like someone had wrapped fry-wire around every little bone and tendon in it, and I skittered over the metal plating like water on a hot griddle. In a moment I was free of the claustrophobic confines of the collapsed portion of tunnel and I couldn't help a split second of relief as my lungs instinctively filled with air. That didn't last long. I was forcibly flipped to my back as another thing grabbed my left leg. Then another grabbed my right hand, the one with Jericho in it, and I got my first look at the new demon of my own personal hell.

It looked at first glance like a mass of tentacles with a beak in the middle. Then my eyes focused properly and I saw it for what it really was. It was a mass of entrails. Mostly intestines, with other bits I never saw clearly enough to identify. They slithered and twisted and writhed over each other like a nest of snakes, questing up the walls and spreading toward me on the deck, the walls, the overhead. They wrapped my limbs spiraling up further and pulling me along the floor to its center.

What I had taken for a beak was a skull. A human skull. Not clean bone, still with plenty of flesh left on it. The eye sockets burned with small glyphs and I could see bloody tear trails leading down past the empty nasal cavity to the mouth. Whatever made this thing hadn't thought a human jaw could do the job. What looked like hands, flayed at the tips of the fingers and sharpened into jagged points, had been attached, forming a pair of grasping, clutching jaws. A length of intestine spilled from the mouth like a swollen tongue and thrashed about erratically. I think the thing that bothered me the most was the noise though.

It was... moaning. Like a man whose tongue had been ripped out. An agonized, melancholy moan. I don't know how it even made the noise, but it did. It keened its low sound as it

120

dragged me closer and threw a loop of some poor cosmonaut's guts at my left hand. That snapped me out of the horror of seeing the thing and I slashed with my a-knife, parting the slimy tentacle with no resistance. The note of its moaning changed slightly, and that appendage slipped back, leaving a trail of offal behind it. Even through the filters on my helmet, the smell... the smell was something I can't even begin to describe. I don't think I'll try.

No sooner was that one gone than half a dozen more lengths of tissue launched themselves out to land wetly on the torso of my suit and begin slithering the rest of the way up my body. I slashed with the a-knife, cutting my torso free, then my right hand. I couldn't use Jericho in here though, just the overpressure could kill me. So slashed like a maniac with my little knife as the monster continued to slither closer and throw out ropes made from the flesh of innocents to entangle me. The severed portions seemed to stay dead, but there was no end to the new loops of tissue. I cut two from my right arm and three wrapped my left leg. I cut those and two slipped around my torso, and all the while I inched closer to that evil, clutching maw. I kicked with my good leg but it did little good, and the bad leg was well and truly fucked now. It burned in my awareness even through the distraction of the fight.

The thing continued to moan miserably, and the shorter length of intestine it used for a tongue darted at me frantically. I started to gain a little leeway by slashing with abandon, and I opened up a gap between us, for a moment. Then it revealed the trap it had let me lay for myself. The severed portions of entrails that had begun to pile up in the tunnel moved of their own volition, surging up around me in a crushing grip of reeking offal

121

and carrion. The shreds of what had once been innocent people slithered up around my waist, and for some reason in that split second, it hit me the pure evil of doing this to people. It hit me that these people had families who would never know what had happened, and would wish they didn't know if they ever found out. As the grasp of the carrion tightened, I heard that moan for what it was:

Pure, elemental suffering.

A soul, no, souls, trapped in a hell they hadn't earned. Whoever was used to make this... Abomination... was still in there, in some way. More than anything, more than the smell or feeling of innards sliding around me, that made me feel sick. I felt pressure in my head, and another sound that I didn't recognize until later as my own roar of rage. My legs bunched under me and my bad ankle screamed in pain as I flung myself into the center of the writhing mass of organs. The finger-mouth froze for a split second in what seemed like surprise, but the tongue-thing shot straight at my face. I managed to duck my head and it slapped into the crown of my helmet, wriggling and writhing frantically. Then my a-knife, held in a reverse grip, slashed through both orbitals of the skull, destroying the glyphs in the eye sockets. The entire mass seemed to be sucked into the dark cavity of the skull for a moment, then it exploded outward and I blacked out.

...

The *Maneki-neko* was eerie. My route to the cargo hold took me past several berthings. I swept them for crew. They were all empty but they were clearly lived in. The captain clearly ran a

122

tight ship, as evidenced by the neat racks and lockers. The ship was clearly lived in though, and used. Some hygiene stuff was out in the heads, boots and vac suits were laid out. None of the crew were present though. Just their kit. The maid ladder passed down through the mess deck at one point. It was clean. Nothing but condiments and the small snacks cooks often liked to leave out for crew to grab on the way to or from a shift. It just didn't seem like the kind of place that had just been through an emergency. To all appearances it was simply a ship between shifts. I made it all the way to the cargo hold air lock without finding any crew. Standard procedure was to call it in before entering any space with an active casualty, so I clocked my comm as I hit the pressurization cycle for the airlock.

"Artie, Harper. I'm entering the casualty space now, no crew found yet. Over."

There was a fuzz of static for a moment, and Cobb's signal was rough when it came through.

"Rog... -at, Harper... clear to ent... --go hold. No cr... here eith--" I shook my head. Somethings will never change, and the fact that a metal ship shreds radio signals is one of them. It was just a fact of the job for us, and we were used to working around it. I had gotten the gist of Cobb's message though, so I swung the airlock door open, stepped through, and resealed it. I checked my seals and air system one more time, then hit the equalize button on the far bulkhead. A low rumble bounced around the compartment as the pumps activated, then muted until I could only feel the pumps through my boots as the last of the air was evacuated from the space.

The outer door swung open without a sound, and I stepped through into the hold. The hold was dark, unlike the rest of the ship. My lamp swept across stacks of metal crates and some loose chunks of ore. That seemed uncharacteristically sloppy. A ship like this would usually carve into asteroids following rich metal deposits, then separate the valuable metal and ore from the rubble outside the ship. There were plenty of reasons most people didn't want rock dust and gravel on a ship. I swept my lamp across the shards of stone. They might be scattered a bit more closely towards the aft end of the hold. It might be something to check on.

After I take care of that pressure leak, I thought to myself.

Wilkins had pointed me towards the starboard side of the hold, so I turned left and clanked my way over to the hull. I swept my lamp over the bulkhead, but I couldn't make out the breach from where I stood. I began picking my way down, scanning the deck as well as the hull. It was often easier to spot something that had moved towards a leak during depressurization than it was to spot the hole itself. Most of the time in a casualty of that kind, the hole would be smaller than my palm. It takes less than we tend to think to be a major problem. I passed row after row of stacked crates, like a labyrinthine maze of narrow alleys on a moonless night. Walking past openings like that always gave me the creeps a bit, like I couldn't help but expect something to be coming down the row at me.

About three quarters of the way back I spotted a sign: an empty crate had tumbled onto its side and skidded across the deck. I stood at the end of the scuffs on the deck, aimed my lamp at the crate, and swept it straight up.

Gotcha, fucker. There was a circular hole in the metal, about as wide as my spread hand, maybe six or seven feet high. I picked my way over the crates to the hull. When I looked back at it, something at the edge of my lamp's beam caught my eye. I panned the light over to it. I felt my face settle into a frown.

Another one?

I slid the beam further down the hull. Another, and another... There were half a dozen of them at least. The shape seemed somewhat familiar. It was almost like...

Like they had a shootout in here.

This job was starting to get to a level of weird I seriously didn't like. I turned to look forward again, some of the crates glinting red and orange in the flash of lamplight.

Wait, I thought. I panned the light off the crates. The glints of color remained. I switched off the lamp and waited a minute for my eyes to adjust. Then I slowly turned around, scanning the space.

There you are...

There was a faint glow emanating from the aft corner of the hold, on the port side. I weaved my way through the stacks of cargo. Some had been toppled, and something crunched underneath the exoskeleton's boots. I looked down.

Gravel?

That was weird. I looked up, towards the source of the light. The bits of broken rock seemed to be strewn more heavily in that direction.

Some crazy bastard still working?

I moved toward the corner slowly. Something about this boat had my teeth on edge. I came around the end of the stack of crates and saw...

A rock?

It was a smooth, oblate rock about the same height as a man, resting on several banged-up crates. It was clearly the source of the broken fragments of rock; stones as big as my fist were piled up underneath it. I couldn't see the broken side as it was facing away from me, but it was clearly the source of that molten-iron light. I crunched my way around the bizarre installation and laid eyes on the source of the light:

An odd mark crawled across the surface of the stone, flowing with the strange light. The rock had been crudely carved away to show every twisting curve and sharp angle of the symbol clearly. I could see discarded power tools atop the pile of rubble. The way the rock was staged made it look like...

An altar?

I didn't like the symbol. It made me feel ill. Odd thoughts started to crawl across my mind, like when something scuttles across your skin as you're falling asleep. I didn't like it, but for some reason I wasn't looking away. I couldn't bring myself to move my eyes. When I tried, the strange susurrus of invasive thoughts seemed to get louder. I started to get scared. I couldn't make my feet move. I couldn't look away. In fact, I realized, I had taken a step *closer* to the ancient rock and its strange mark. I lost myself for a second, and I was closer still. I could reach out and touch it at that point. That sparked something and I clenched my jaw. The lines seemed like they were moving. Writhing and spiraling in a bizarre, four-dimensional revolution. I could feel myself groaning, or maybe even screaming, but I couldn't hear it over the noise in my own head. My left hand reached out, clad in the metal exoskeleton of my casualty suit. I gasped.

The suit!

I struggled to close my fingers in a specific pattern; after three years of almost living in that suit, the controls were muscle memory. I struggled against the tide of distracting thoughts and forced my fingers into a specific pattern. I could feel the *chunk-chunk* of the tool I needed readying itself.

Come on, come on... All I needed to do was move my left index finger like I was pulling a trigger. Just a little bit. But it wouldn't move. I couldn't make it move. I thought of moving closer, and the pressure in my mind eased slightly. So I used that. I lurched forward, left hand still extended, finger still trying to

127

curl. My hand landed on the rough stone with all my weight behind it, and my finger moved. I felt a powerful *hiss-clunk* and the nail gun planted a nail the size of my finger in the stone deep enough to send cracks skittering across its surface. The symbol dimmed and flickered. It didn't go out, but it was enough. I could *move.* My right hand swept up from my waist, drawing my service pistol in one smooth arc. I squeezed the trigger. Then I did it again, and again. I didn't stop until the last flicker of light left the glyph. Then I fell to my knees in the rubble.

Chapter Twelve

Since time immemorial, since before man took to the stars, in the days when the only expanse we sailed was the seas of our ancestral home on Terra, sailors of all kinds have had a tradition of making decisions they regret before a bad wake-up. I've been a cosmonaut of one kind or another my entire adult life, and I know what a bad wake-up is. After coming to in a cramped service corridor filled with loops of rotting intestines, on a derelict ship full of monsters out to get me, I reserve the right to claim the worst wake-up in the long and sordid history of bad wakeups. My head was pounding and my right shoulder was throbbing in addition to my ankle.

Shit. My ankle...

I didn't know how long I'd been out, but my chem lamp had dimmed considerably and my ankle had stiffened. I could barely move it and I knew that without the initial burst of adrenaline that had accompanied the injury and my flight from the monsters it would be doubly painful to test it now. Unfortunately I didn't have the luxury of taking it easy; I was still at the bottom of a ship full of monstrosities, alone and with no help coming. Ever. I needed to get the plans I'd crawled into this damned machine for, and find a way to scuttle the ship and get off this deathtrap alive at the same time.

I had dropped my a-knife when I blacked out, and I had to spend a few minutes sifting through the remains of *Alea's* poor, damned crew before I could find it. I wasn't leaving it behind for anything, for one simple reason more than any other: knives don't run out of ammo. I cast a few shaky glances at the epicenter of the explosion of gore, thinking of those baleful glyphs burning in an innocent man's skull. I couldn't see any remnants of the skull or its glyphs. Somehow that didn't set my mind at ease as I clambered back down the tunnel. I wanted to get out of here, get somewhere different and try to throw these things off my track, but I still didn't have the information I needed.

Under my circumstances... Without preparation, I'd be another component for whatever fucked up monstrosity my enemies wanted to make next. I refused to be stripped down for parts and turned into some godforsaken homunculus to torment the living. I reached the bottleneck again and surveyed it with no small amount of apprehension. I pictured a candle again, a flame bursting into existence on its wick, and told myself I only had to be calm until the candled burned down. Then I wriggled into the tight gap again. More slowly this time, and when I felt the walls of the tunnel pressing against my back and chest again. I pictured my candle and slowly shifted my body until I could squeeze through. I slid through the tightest spots without getting stuck. After the second time it happened, I realized that the fluids from the monster were still on my suit, acting as a slight lubricant. I gave a dry bark of a laugh at that.

Then I wriggled through the last crushed portion of the tunnel and flopped out the other side. My ankle connected with an edge in the metal on the way down, and I bit pack a grunt of pain. Then I lit a different candle in my mind's eye, red for pain this time, and told myself another lie. I only had to work through the pain until the candle burned out. Then I could rest. I swallowed the pain and kept going, crawling through the remains of the tunnel like a rat seeking a familiar burrow.

There.

At last, I saw a hatch. That indicated a sealed space, which is where the microfilm backups would be kept. I heaved with my arms, ignoring the throb of strained tendons in my right shoulder, and I slid the rest of the way to the hatch. I ran my hands around it, trying to find the access handle that would allow me to get to the information I so desperately needed, but it seemed to have been torn off at some point. Deliberately or in the same event that collapsed the maintenance crawlway, I had no way of knowing. It didn't even slow me down. With my one tangible goal within reach, I was half-mad with determination to get what I needed. I whipped my a-knife from its sheath without really thinking about it and flicked it open in the confined space. It had taken years of practice for me to be willing to even try something like that in tight quarters.

I hacked at the hatch with more aggression than skill, taking chips out of the dogs and hinges almost randomly. When I had first acquired the knife, I had thought a subatomic edge would let me cut through anything. That turned out to be very wrong. The blade still has to have some thickness. That thickness means that if you want to cut something, you need to displace the material you're cutting by the width of the blade. So while the knife is technically capable of cutting through, say, a ship's hull, it's

131

not practically possible because no-one has the strength to force apart the metal of the hull.

Those limitations very probably had a lot to do with why the technology wasn't actively pursued in the modern day. I knew I wouldn't be able to just cut through the hatch, so I shaved off slivers of metal from the hinges and the dogs holding it closed, whittling them down like a bored boy might a dry twig. It didn't take long to carve the hatch free and pry it off with my simplest tool, the humble crowbar I kept in my tool bag. The seal on the hatch popped, and I stuffed my crowbar back in my tool bag. I carefully wrapped my fingers around the edge of the hatch and slowly pried it off. I managed to get it off the sealing edge without making a racket or dropping it, but as I went to set the hatch to the side it caught on the stub of one of the hinges and one edge slipped free of my hand. The corner of the heavy chunk of metal slammed into the deck with a deafening crash, and my stomach dropped with it. I dropped my head to the deck for a second, frustrated by my clumsiness.

The fatigue and injuries were piling up. I was starting to make stupid mistakes. That was a fairly bad sign given how far I still had to go to get the job done, but I didn't dwell on it too long. There was no point.

"Through the thorns to the stars," I whispered as I crawled through the hatchway.

The inside of the data vault was even more labyrinthine than the crawlways leading to it. This section of the ship had never been meant for human travel. Maintenance techs would crack the hatch I had just ripped off and send in a wire-controlled drone if anything in here needed attention. That was mainly to prevent people from contaminating the pristine data machinery with any sweat, dust, or, in my case, blood and every biological contaminant known to man. It was also because the spaces between the racks of data cassettes were tight. Each cassette consisted of a ribbon of microscopically thin and incredibly narrow graphene. The graphene was essentially a microscopic, extremely durable version of an ancient film reel.

The ribbon could be etched with lines of text and simple diagrams. The one I needed would mostly look like screenshots of *Alea's* rector OS the last time a backup was made. A cassette could be run through virtually any reader consisting of a light source and what amounted to a large magnifier and amplifier, and the images projected. It is an archaic, low-resolution, but incredibly durable way to store data if you absolutely want to make sure they don't get wiped. My wrist unit was mostly trashed, but the reader would still function well enough to read some plans. I just had to get to the engineering stack and get the right cassette. I hauled my way through the cramped space. The stacks were arranged like hexagonal towers of cassettes holding up a cramped ceiling, making it cramped, difficult to turn or maneuver, and disturbingly exposed all at once.

A maintenance bot would be able to crawl circles around me in here, easily slipping between the pillars that hampered me. The space between my shoulder blades seemed to itch when I had that thought, and had to focus on my candle image and take a few deep breaths before I kept searching. The stacks were labeled only with drone-code, visual markers used by drones to identify different sections. English wasn't used because that would almost be like giving me a damn break, so I had to muddle through with my order-in-a-restaurant level of understanding in the machine language, garnered years ago and rarely used since. I passed dozens of towers, most either storage for old tapes or blank tapes awaiting imprinting. The whole time, that itch in between my shoulder blades continued, and I thought I could hear the skittering of metallic servos. The third time I heard something I wrenched my body around, absolutely sure something had been moving towards my back. Nothing. I started to move on, and then something caught my eye. A drone-code glyph was staring at me from a foot away, mocking me with its simple presence:

bioHaz/trnspt.Lg/Cdvrs

Biohazard Transport Log; Cadavers. *Alea* had been hauling bodies from one of the world-cities for reclamation in some po-dunk system, or if they croaked with enough money, to be buried on some idyllic hillside. I dropped my head to the deck. I couldn't even feel scared at that point, to be honest with you. I was just... Tired. No, not tired; weary. I was weary. I'd been keeping myself going by thinking that I had a chance. If the only people who had been. . . Reused were the members of *Alea's* crew, I could have made a good run for it: there were bound to be gaps in their net where I could slip back to *Erebus* and start hauling ass to the other end of the cosmos. But even a fraction of *Alea's* cargo hold could have held thousands of cadavers.

It was routine to ship cadavers from stations or over-crowded worlds to be dealt with elsewhere in the galaxy. There could have been tens of thousands of bodies on this ship that my enemies could use, whatever they were.

God damn it. That's why they took this ship.

It was the question I hadn't stopped to ask myself since everything went to hell: Why the *Alea*? Of all the ships transiting the galaxy in that period of time, what was special about this one? It clear from what I'd seen that they needed to use organic parts to make their... puppets. I didn't know why or how they made these constructs, but... Where better to get bodies than a grave ship? I remembered Bly's words; *To make everywhere like this, I think,* and the truth hit me. *Alea* was a plague ship. That was the right way to think of it. If it reached an inhabited system it would spread the same carnage there, and who knew how much further?

I had been thinking of this as a scuttle-and-run mission, a desperate bid for survival. But that wasn't right. This was a quarantine mission. It was contagion control, nothing more. I just had to make sure all the rats went down with the ship. I wasn't sure what that made me. I tried not to think about it.

Chapter Thirteen

Once I had the cassettes I needed, I scrambled back to the hatch and jammed the door in place as best I could. Then I started scrolling through *Alea*'s plans on the cracked screen of my wrist unit. There were a huge number of frames to move through. I saw routine maintenance logs, a mention of someone attempting some emergency repairs inside the reactor after the crash... It didn't take me long to find what I needed: the reactor specifications. There was no grace to what I was planning; any gorilla can break something. I did need some specifics though-- make, model, year of the reactor. Although the protocol was always called the Hail Mary, it was actually more of an approach. Technically, what I was planning on doing wasn't technically a Hail Mary. That term referred to starting the reactor or sub-drives without certain safeguards in place. It was a last-ditch effort to reach civilization again before you ran out of air. That could work, but it wasn't a guaranteed bet; safeguards exist for a reason.

What I was going to do was use the Hail Mary to start the reactor, then deliberately leverage the fact that the safeguards were off to turn the controlled fusion reaction happening in the core into a fusion bomb by tricking the reactor into believing there was an impossible demand for power: a subspace dive leading out of the known galaxy. Without the cutoffs in place, the reactor would attempt to meet the near-infinite request for power. The resulting explosion would immolate the *Alea* and anyone within a sizable radius, and the run-up to critical should--theoretically--give me enough time to get off the ship before it blew. For any of that to work though, someone would have to have made a Hail Mary protocol when the ship was still functioning. I scanned one frame after another, speeding up slightly as they slid by without giving me the information I needed. I flicked past a slide, then backtracked.

There you are...

The protocol list for the reactor had something buried deep in a sub directory: one item titled *Ave Maria*. Hail Mary. The game was on. I scanned the slide, committing what I needed to memory. I felt the burn of satisfaction; I had something these monsters wouldn't know about--they had never left anyone alive and independent to try something like this. Now that I had my weapon, I turned to the deck plans. It wasn't great news. There were only three ways for a human to get from the engineering level up to the crew level where I had docked *Erebus*: the main lift, which was no longer an option, the emergency ladder, which was a death trap, and a cargo lift for moving parts in and out of the engineering space, on the port side of the engineering deck.

Damn.

I had hoped that there would be more than that. I had known about the two lifts, but I couldn't climb up the old shaft even if the big monster from earlier didn't catch up to me. The ladder was a straight shot for something like forty meters. So all the downsides of the lift without the speed. That meant that the only viable option was to make my way to the cargo elevator and hope that it wasn't a trap. Which not only meant I had to backtrack through the entire engineering bay, but also that I would have to cross the entire beam of the ship to get back to the starboard side, where *Erebus* was waiting. I searched quickly for any other way up. No dice; I clicked from one map to the next. Chutes for the maintenance drones, a few air ducts that were not appropriately sized for crawling... Nothing I could get through. I flicked to another plan, and clenched a fist in frustration.

There were two problems. The first was that there wasn't a direct route from where I was to the reactor. The reactor was almost dead center in the cavernous engineering space. Although I was only a little aft of the reactor and to the starboard side of the space, the direct route there was blocked by the hulking mass of the sub-drive. That made sense, since the location of the sub-drive within the ship didn't matter much to its function, and it was logical to put the single largest consumer of power for that reactor where you could move the power with minimal loss. People tend to get the engines and sub-drive mixed up if they're not familiar with the systems.

The explanation that stuck with me was that if the engines filled the same role as they did on an old-fashioned submarine, then the sub-drive would be the ballast system that let it change its buoyancy. Shipwrights rarely consider crew convenience when designing propulsion systems, sadly. Their focus is on performance and how to get a lot of very complicated machines to work together relatively well. To be fair, the personnel and cargo lifts were both straight lines from the reactor's control dais. The simple fact was that I was currently in a part of the space almost no one ever visited.

The second problem was that the aft bulkhead of the main engineering space was a primary vacuum barrier to the main hold. The main hold was a little less than a kilometer in diameter, and had originally been something like seven kilometers long, probably something like three or four now. Ships this size almost never pressurized the main hold; they didn't have enough air and there wouldn't be any point anyway. What that meant for me was that there was a wall of very solid metal on the aft end of the compartment with hard vacuum beyond it.

The problem was that there was absolutely nowhere to go aft of the engineering deck. There was nothing but a foot and a half of metal and a whole lot of hard cold beyond that. I dropped my head to my chest and thought for a second, switching off my reader. There was no other way: the cargo lift was my only option. The ladder was an absolute death trap and skipped several levels at a time, I had no way of getting back up the lift shaft I had taken to get down to the Engineering deck, and there were no other ways up. The perfect place to trap an overconfident investigator if you wanted to make sure he got dead. It was easy to isolate on purpose: although the engines were located at the rear of the ship, there were still plenty of reasons you'd want to put a cork in this space and bottle it up for a bit. The silver lining was that if I made it to the reactor and set the timer on this bomb, it would be a quick sprint to the cargo elevator. I was pulled from my thoughts by a noise at the edge of my hearing.

What's that?

It was... clicking.

Shit.

It was distant, but it was coming from both ends of the tunnel. I checked the cylinder on Jericho.

One shot left, old buddy. Better make this one count.

I checked my a-knife. Mostly to make sure it was still there, since it would take a nuke to actually damage it.

I listened to the clicking.

"Come on, James," I said to myself. "You gotta die sometime, no sense getting whiny about it."

Hard to believe my career as a motivational speaker never took off after that gem.

Chapter Fourteen

I channeled the mindset of the tunnel rat one more time then. I slipped through the tight spot like I'd been born to do it, fueled by adrenaline and eager to be moving again, to be doing something about my situation. My mind felt like it narrowed to an edge of focus. Adrenaline has a way of focusing the mind like that. Once there's an enemy, a task, a job to be done, your body unlocks a lot. In my experience, fear is like water: It wants to be moving, have a direction. Make it build up without an outlet and it will blow your state of mind apart from the inside.

I slid through the maintenance tunnel gracelessly and painfully. I tried to maintain as much economy of motion as I could. I held back just enough to avoid making a huge racket. I suspected that their knowledge of my position wasn't perfect, and there was no sense being sloppier than I had to be already. Besides, my ankle and shoulder could only move so fast. The clicking was getting louder as I got closer to the exit. I paused at one of the last turns and listened.

They're out there, all right...

I thought for a second, then dug out my fry wire. I clipped a piece the length of my finger off, then reached around my back with my left hand and popped a canister free. I stuck the fry-wire to the canister, and got ready to light the stick. I took a single shaky breath, then pushed off. I slipped around that last corner, Jericho in hand, and slithered down the final stretch of the crawl way like one of the nightmares I was fighting. I saw shifting flickers of light outside the range of my ever-dimming chem lamp, and I lit the fuse on the fry-wire. Then I tossed the canister out the hole and whipped my a-knife out with my free hand. There was a pause, a clatter, then a huge, hollow *THOOMP.*

A blast of pressure shoved me back and the thermometer in my helmet warned me of a temperature spike. Shrapnel from the canister rattled around the inside of the tunnel and I slid out into a pile of jumbled drone parts and severed body parts. My improvised grenade had been nothing more than one of my water canisters and enough fry-wire to vaporize it into blast of pressurized steam. Cooling had done in the last batch of these little cretins and I had suspected they might not react any better to a temperature fluctuation in the other direction. I could still hear more on the way, but I had bought myself a head start. I hauled myself to my feet, feeling like an ant scuttling around among the cyclopean machines of *Alea's* too-still heart.

I ran at a lopsided lope, the fresh surge of adrenaline overwhelming the pain in my ankle through brute hormonal force and urging me onward. There was a certain amount of calm resolve then, knowing I only had one way out. For some reason, knowing I only had one option, and it was either succeed or die... It held a certain amount of calm for me, if not peace.

Shipboard combat was and always will be a nightmare of uncontrollable variables though. I pictured some of the plans I

144

had etched into my mind's eye in the few minutes I had spent studying them and overlapped them with my memories from my previous mad dash about the engineering space, and skidded around a corner to my left. I was outpacing the clicking, but not by much. My memory is trained, not perfect, so I had to go all the way to the rear bulkhead so that I could use it as a guide across the rest of the engineering space. There was no way to memorize the entire jumbled map of this deck, so I had only memorized what I needed: the turns to get to the rear bulkhead from the data core. From there it was a straight shot to the reactor up the centerline of the ship. From the reactor it I just needed to make it to the port side of the space and I would be at the lift. There wasn't much time to get where I needed to go, but there's never an abundance of time to be stupid either. Getting lost in this maze of machinery would be a death sentence.

As I loped along the meandering corridor between machines to the rear bulkhead, the clicking and chittering of the horde of drones grew steadily louder from behind me. They were coming from the forward part of the space. That wasn't ideal. I scanned the walls of the metal canyon in front of me.

I should be getting--there!

I juked around one piece of machinery and half-vaulted, half-stumbled over some conduit that was laying across the walkway. A smooth expanse of metal rose up in front of me: the rear bulkhead of the cavernous room. I slid around the corner in a right turn, slamming my left shoulder against the bulkhead and almost gutting myself with my a-knife in the process. I shoved off to run along the wall and immediately snagged my bad ankle on

145

an awkward semicircular protrusion where the rear bulkhead met the deck of the engineering bay. I shot off along the bulkhead with the kind of speed only a flight from death can give you, heedless of the growing pain in my leg and the ache in my shoulder that were trying to slow me down to a crawl.

I had to jump over several more of those odd protrusions, which were just wide enough that I couldn't comfortably leap them. I stumbled over them inelegantly, keeping the worst of the stress on my good leg whenever I could. Something about the bulky metal blocks bounced off my focus, very nearly entering my conscious, but then it was gone and I had bigger problems. They were catching up. The noise was loud. Louder than the first time, and I had survived that because I had been extraordinarily lucky and managed to stumble upon a coolant tank at just the right time. I suspected that by the time the day was done I would end up using my life's entire allotment of luck, and maybe some from my next life as well. It was a decisively sub-optimal day up to that point. I hauled myself down the bulkhead with increasing speed as the chittering, clicking tumult rose behind me.

There.

The turn towards the reactor. I heaved my body around to the right and into the open walkway that would lead me to the main reactor. I was now running directly forward, up the center of the ship towards the bow. I couldn't see the control dais off to the port side of the power plant, but I knew it would be there. That dais was where I would need to be to initiate the Hail Mary protocol and set the reactor on a course to self-destruct. From there it should be a straight line athwartships to the cargo elevator, which was located along the center of the port bulkhead of the space. I sprinted as best I could up the deck, focusing all my energy on churning my burning legs and ignoring the pain of my joints and lungs. The horde of drones seemed to be moving parallel to my course now. I could hear their mismatched legs skittering and clicking on the alloy of the deck plates even over my own heaving breath. In the distance off to my left, I heard something grinding into action, some piece of machinery on the port side of the space that must have been on its own power. The short range of my fading chem lamp meant that it came as a surprise when I burst into the center of the level.

I could dimly see the reactor across some twenty meters of open deck. It was a cylindrical tower of white ceramic and grey alloy, sitting alone in a circular space amongst the machines the powered and managed the *Alea*. The control dais was a vague outline ahead of me and to my left, and I veered towards it. After the first step I knew something was wrong. I felt a rumble through the deck plates and something glinted to my left, in my peripheral vision. My eyes snapped to the source of light.

Gods above...

Bly might have been a rat, but had been honest about at least one thing: the big one was *big*.

Chapter Fifteen

Rattle. Thump. Pause. Rattle. I caught my first really clear glimpse of the monstrosity. A dozen hands slapped down from around the corner of one of the giant machines in front of me. Flayed and skinless, they were more shredded meat and splintered bone than arms at this point. They left bloody streaks wherever they touched, speckled with marrow and the remains of fingernails that had been torn from the unfortunate remains. They flexed, scrabbling at the deck even as more appeared to grip the side of the machinery, then heaved. THUMP. The monstrosity heaved itself into the open space surrounding the reactor. It was as wide as a man was tall and shaped like a worm: a parasite scaled up to match *Alea's* size.

It was formed entirely, as far as I could see, out of limbs. Specifically, arms. Thousands and thousands of them, seething and grasping and writhing. Each had a glyph blazing on its surface. The rattling I had heard was the limbs slapping down to grab the deck and heave the titanic abomination across the deck, hauling all at once and lurching forward in jerky stops. The limbs on the outside were pulped but still grasped at everything around the creature. It gave the impression that the poor souls who had been used in its creation were all desperately trying to heave themselves out of the abomination they had been turned into.

The inner row spiraled in a nauseating kind of fractal into a pulsing orifice, limbs spliced with jagged shards of metal to serve as razor sharp fangs. The hands near the quivering not-mouth were constantly feeding rubbish and the remains of the drone swarm I had flash frozen into the gaping hole, and the offerings were just as frequently rejected and kicked back to the deck. The motion reminded me unpleasantly of a toddler exploring the world by putting things in their mouth carelessly. Then the thing stopped. I mean stopped. Not one digit moved. That awful orifice turned to face me. I could see where my earlier blind shots at the abomination had charred and destroyed parts of it. If these things felt pain, I had probably caused it plenty. We stood there, frozen, for a moment, staring at each other across the shadows and detritus.

Then hands all around the body started spasming, slamming limply against the mass of flesh in a grotesque parody of applause. The arms on one side, then the other started slapping down, hauling it across the deck towards me, and I could see that the thing must be thirty meters long or better. I drew Jericho stiffly as I watched death approach. My mind raced. There had been an idea, thinking about my route over here. something I had skipped past in my desperate dash for the reactor. The run along the rear bulkhead flashed through my mind, and it clicked. The aft bulkhead.

I hauled myself into motion, right arm screaming and left ankle barely holding, running back the way I had come. I could feel the rampaging devil behind me shaking the deck as it got closer, bearing down on me with every grotesque lurch of its body. Pain notwithstanding, that's the fastest I've ever moved in my life. There's fear, and then there's *monster-right-behind-you* fear. I only needed to make it a few meters, but it wasn't going to happen. My lead hadn't been enough. And then I ran into the new swarm. It was just a few stragglers at first, launching themselves at me. I felt impacts on my ribs and legs, small weights tenaciously trying to penetrate my suit and perforate my body. I felt the *rattle, THUMP* close enough that it made me stumble just as the aft bulkhead came into view. My eyes slipped up the smooth metal until they locked on what I needed, and then my hand came up.

I squeezed the trigger. The round streaked away from Jericho like the wrath of God toppling the walls of the titular bastion. A line of fire blazed into the target I had selected: The bulkhead separating me and my foe from the emptiness of space that lurked like a hungry devil. Specifically, the spot where the coolant tanks had been just a few hours earlier. The bulkhead screamed and bulged outwards, but it didn't give. The creature was closing in behind me. I fired my sixth and final round.

And the walls came tumbling down.

The bulkhead had already been weakened by the flood of coolant I had unleashed previously. It never stood a chance. At that point all hell... well. Hell seemed pretty loose already thereabouts things really kicked into gear. The tortured bulkhead screamed as it gave way under the cumulative air pressure in the engineering bay, and likely the rest of the ship. The massive machines had to be brought in somehow and moving them in parts wasn't always an option. This space had been open to the void while the ship was being constructed and then closed up and sealed shut. The intent was that it was not to be opened again until the ship needed to have some major machinery replaced.

Everything was put in place and the bulkhead sealed so little trace was left. The semicylindrical protrusions I had been stumbling over were the hinges for the "bulkhead". I realized as I bounced down the floor towards the rent in the metal of the ship that my plan had a flaw or nine, but the die had been cast and the big nasty was tumbling with me so I called it my win. I tucked my limbs in tight as I hurtled down the deck like a stone kicked by a kid. I slammed my shoulder and ankle more than once. The metal must have been more affected by the coolant than I had realized; the tear went almost down to the deck. I tumbled through without any more major injuries, and then I was drifting in the void of *Alea*'s cargo bay.

Weightlessness is an extremely disorienting sensation, particularly when you're introduced to it abruptly, and I was acutely aware that I was emitting light from my chem lamp, which would act as a beacon in the pitch-black void. I gently twisted my head around, starting a spin, and I realized that I was completely devoid of senses. No hearing, because there was no air. No sight, because nothing was within the range of my chem lamp. As far as I could see, hear, smell, or touch, I was completely alone in a perfect void. The dim light from my chem lamp had the effect of illuminating my body and therefore casting the rest of the void into deeper contrast. There are a lot of things all spacers and cosmonauts fear. I was currently reliving the most common, and a personal favorite: I had spaced myself. I felt my breathing start to pick up and my heart begin to pound at the thought of drifting helplessly until my air ran out, unable to do anything at all to save myself. A slow, creeping death that only had one way out most of the time: ending it early.

I could feel the fear setting in, and I went back to my image of the candles. I focused on the image of that flame, burning slower and slower the closer it got to the base of the candle, and my heart rate stopped climbing at least. Panic was the ultimate enemy now. That and the enormous monstrosity that could almost certainly see my chem lamp blazing like a beacon if it had any capacity at all for sight. I can't explain the feeling, other than... Helplessness. Absolute helplessness. I couldn't move. I couldn't control my movement. I couldn't get air if I started to run out. I was completely restrained by... nothing. By the complete absence of anything around me. I don't know how long I drifted. Time stretched out, and I lost track. I drifted, as I thought. marking time was difficult; my forearm unit had finally given up completely in the hard vacuum of the hold. Minutes, I think. probably not hours. It didn't matter. I drifted, possibilities swirling through my mind. The upside was that there was no reason to think that the big one could maneuver any better out here than I could.

Sometimes you have to clear the board to wi—I slammed into something, hard.

I gasped a breath into my helmet. Of course I would land on the bad shoulder. I was already rebounding, drifting away. I acted without thinking. My right arm whipped my a-knife out of its sheath and stabbed at whatever I had hit. The blade pierced into what felt like metal, and I hauled myself in until my helmet *thunked* against the object. I took a deep breath, eyes closed, and focused on the pain candle while my shoulder stopped screaming. Then I opened my eyes and looked straight into the eyes of a corpse. I jerked a bit.

Once, that would have bothered me. Now... now it was almost a relief to see a dead body still intact, and not corrupted into some kind of weapon. The object I had hit was a cryopod. The kind that keeps people on ice after they've died, instead of before. I found myself looking into the eyes of a young man, perhaps nineteen or twenty, maybe younger. I suppose I should have taken a moment to lament the kid, but frankly I was just glad to have something to anchor myself to, a solid object I could use as a launching point. I held tight to the a-knife and wedged my fingers into the gap of the lid, then scanned the absolute darkness for anything else, craning my head around to check three hundred and sixty degrees around me.

Nothing.

I remember wondering if the darkness was what a drowning sailor might have experienced as he was pulled into the briny hell of old Terra. Hypothetically, if I were to jump, I had very good chanced of encountering the skin of the ship after a few minutes of drifting. The *Alea* was only a kilometer wide, so if I pushed off at the speed of a slow walk then I would collide with one of the sides of the ship quickly. Unless I was unlucky and launched myself straight out the back of the destroyed ship. Given how the day had gone, I wasn't feeling optimistic.

"Shit," I said to myself eloquently. Then I frowned, unsatisfied.

154

"Shit, hell, damn, fuck, and balls."

That was slightly better. I maintain I had as much justification for profanity as any man ever did in that moment, and probably more. I paused there, clinging to a coffin like a rat clinging to flotsam, and struggled to think through the pain and exhaustion. The inactivity was the worst part. It made the threat and fear dull to my body, and I started to feel like the danger had passed. I blearily tried to think of a way to improve my odds of getting to the inside bulkhead of the hold.

Then I had to drag myself back to reality. The danger hadn't passed. It was, in fact, greater than ever. My air was finite, my displays were out, and even my chem lamp was looking dimmer and dimmer. Think as I might, I couldn't come up with a way to determine the correct direction. Which meant there was only one thing to do. Eighty percent now is worth a hundred percent late. I nodded my thanks at the cadaver for letting me hitch a ride for a few minutes, then peered into the absolute darkness surrounding me. I really had no idea whether I was about to launch myself into the void to die of suffocation or get shredded by bits of the *Alea*, but there was nothing for it.

I picked the direction that seemed best and kicked off. It's amazing the difference a little agency makes. When I hit that pod, I had been in a state of fear because I had no control over my fate. Now, even though I was likely going in the wrong direction, I was a little steadier. Nothing incites panic like complete helplessness. Knowing that I had picked this direction made my situation easier to bear.

I floated for what felt like more hours, but I was using my pain as a reference for the time, paying attention to the ebb and flow of it, and I don't think it was that long before I saw something. In the distance ahead of me I thought I saw something else. Something started to feel very off again, and I realized that I wasn't looking at a bulkhead. Then motes of light shone and sparked over the surface of the thing and my gut dropped. Glyphs. The motes of light on the thing were glyphs. I couldn't wrap my mind around what I was seeing. My eyes strained for a moment, then the glyphs flared and I saw it. My stomach dropped. *Alea* had been carrying bodies. The mortal shells of thousands departed souls. Just like the poor sap I'd just used as a launch pad. They had been used.

It stretched across the entire thousand-meter width of the hold, like a spider web stretching across a pipe. Thousands of threads of charnel and offal had been spun into dizzying fractal patterns. The overall impression was almost like a wall of noise-- sheer volume of sensation impeding my ability to think. The entire thing glittered with glyphs. More by far than had been on the outside of the hull. It almost reminded me of... A brain. Neurons. It drew my eyes towards the center like a black hole drew matter. I have never seen anything that filled me with that kind of dread before or since.

Bly had been a twisted, vile man by the time I killed him, but he was a man. The other things I had seen clearly had some level of intelligence, but it seemed... narrow. Like those monsters could do exactly what they were designed to do, but not much beyond that scope. They were still dangerous, still to be avoided. As I watched, I became aware of movement in the web. There were things crawling along the many strands of the odious formation. Constructs that looked like distended ticks dragging bloated bodies along the threads of the construct. Sigils glowed from within the distended sacs. I saw one, relatively near to me. It dragged its pendulous body behind it until it reached the end of a strand, and then started regurgitating matter, spewing it out like a spider weaving silk. Limbs and entrails slid out of its mouth and were frozen in place with the secretion of some kind of fluid.

My gaze was dragged away from the sight of the monstrous laborer, back to the center. My body continued to drift, beyond my control, but my mind, my sense of self, was dragged inexorably into the center of the symbol. And it was one. One massive glyph. I heard a murmur of strange thoughts at the edge of my awareness, something I hadn't felt in a long, long time. Then I felt the sensation of falling, accelerating towards the center of the vast web at great speed, and everything went black.

Chapter Sixteen

It took me a few minutes to pull myself together. I could feel something wet and warm leaking from my eyes and my nose. It dripped on the faceplate of my helmet as I slumped over the shipping crates and broken stone. I couldn't get a string of thoughts together. One thought just didn't connect right to the next. I'm not sure exactly how long, but eventually my head cleared in a rush. I had a migraine that pounded behind my eyes with every heartbeat and every breath. My thoughts cleared as suddenly as if I had been thrown in ice water though. I blinked at the darkness I around me. My lamp had been switched off at some point. I didn't remember doing it. I flicked the light on and it illuminated another man's face six inches from mine.

I reeled back with a hoarse cry. He didn't follow. It took me a moment to process what I'd seen. The body was slumped over some of the crates. He would have been hidden from my line of sight when I initially came around the corner. Once I had looked at the rock, I wouldn't have noticed him if he'd been doing a jig. I looked back at the face. It was clear why he hadn't moved. Someone had gouged his eyes out. It was hard to look at him. There were ragged lines all over his face. I held my hand out and adjusted my fingers a bit.

Fingernails? Who the fuck does *that?*

159

I stumbled to my feet and hit my comm–this case had gone from "weird" to "get the hell out now".

"Artie, Harper. We need to get out of here boss, this place is fucked, we need to leave." Static.

"...lm down, Har-- what's got... –pset?" I could barely make out what Cob was saying. I started walking. The power of the suit always lent a certain amount of confidence to anybody's stride.

"There's some weird shit here Cobb, some kind of weird cult or something. I've got a body down here. They gouged out his eyes, Cobb, someone gouged out his eyes *with their hands*, man--" I cut myself off when I realized I was rambling.

I made it to the central "avenue" of the hold and turned left; back towards the airlock for the hold. Patching the hold had just gone to the bottom of my priority list. All I was thinking about was the fact that my crew were on this hulk with an unknown number of crazed, asteroid-worshipping cultists. I drew my sidearm as I stumbled up the deck. The dark alleys of the cargo stacks leered at me mockingly. Every time I passed one I had the impression of someone watching me from the side. If anyone was there though, they didn't show themselves. Not then and not when I lurched into the airlock and slammed the control to equalize. I dimly recalled pulling the trigger many times in quick succession in front of the asteroid. I checked my pistol belatedly. I had gone through an entire magazine destroying that rock. Sixty rounds gone in a haze. I reloaded and admonished myself mentally:

Some security, Harper.

If there had been hostiles in the hold, I would have found myself pulling the trigger of an empty gun. There was nothing to be done about it at that point though, so I channeled that frustration into focus. The inner airlock door whooshed open and I slipped out with my pistol held at the low ready. The first thing I noticed was that it was now dark. The beam of my lamp flicked through the darkness in jerky arcs.

"Security check, sound off." That short sentence was one of the few orders I could give on a case. Anybody who heard it was required to check in so that security could verify the status of all the boarding team members. After a few seconds of static the comm clicked. I brought my weapon up to the low ready and moved forward with careful, smooth steps, like I had been taught in boarding school. There was nothing ut static over the radio. I could hear my breathing echoing in my helmet. The pain pulsed behind my eyes.

"Security check, sound off," I tried again. Nothing.

I bounded up the ladder two steps at a time. Wilkins had been headed to the engine room. That was above and aft of the cargo hold. I stepped out of the main ladder well and into the central corridor of the deck. *Maneki-neko* wasn't a big ship. It was only forty meters or so from the lift to the engine room.

I started walking, my head pounding with every step. I winced, and my gaze dropped. When I looked back up, the corridor stretched out in front of me, like it was a tunnel of

161

mirrors. The tunnel extended into infinity, endless series of connecting corridors and hatches repeating until they all converged into a single point of darkness. That point drew me in. It was like space was twisting and writhing there, at the far end of infinity. The distortion rushed towards me, and I yelled involuntarily and jerked my pistol up. My finger was in the trigger well before I got myself under control and lowered the weapon. Then I slammed into something, *hard*. The air *whooshed* out of my lungs and I rocked from side to side as I struggled to pull in a breath. I slid down until my knees hit the deck. That seemed odd. I looked up and I saw that I had slammed, not into the deck, but into the hatch to the engine room. I struggled to my feet and staggered around to look at the lift. I heard someone whisper behind me and I spun, pistol raised.

Nothing but the door. My hands were shaking. My breath was unsteady. I reached out, tentatively, and hit the open button. The door whooshed open and I ran through, into... The cargo hold. I stumbled to a stop and spun around but the door was gone. I was standing in the middle of the cargo hold. I heard whispering again, over my left shoulder, and I saw amber light reflecting off of the stacks of crates.

I turned, slowly, and the space seemed to blur around me, swirling and rearranging itself until I stood in front of the altar again. Something *pulled* at me and I lurched forward, towards the rock. I caught myself on the rock with my left hand and struggled to bring my pistol up. It felt like the gravity had been turned up to nine g's specifically under my gun hand. I growled desperately and hauled the gun up, suit servos overpowering the incredible weight of the weapon. Arm trembling, teeth clenched, I slid my finger into the trigger guard. I felt the hard, flat surface of the trigger under the pad of my index finger. Something caught at the edge of my hearing. It sounded like... My name?

I looked back over my shoulder, but there was nothing there, just the conduit and machinery of the engine room. I startled and spun back to the rock, only it wasn't the rock. It was Wilkins. I had him pinned to a control panel with my left glove. He was straining with both arms to shove my right hand down, but to no avail. My pistol was leveled at his gut. My finger was in the trigger guard. I screamed and stumbled back. I threw the pistol away, under the machinery of the engine room. I dropped my helmet into my hands. My eyes burned. It felt like it had been hours since I first walked into the cargo hold. I could hear Wilkins panting across from me.

"Chuck..." I said hoarsely, "I don't know what's happening to me, man." My cheeks were wet. "I don't know... My head hurts man. I don't know what's happening around here." He didn't say anything, so I continued:

"There's something wrong on this ship, Chuck. Something fucked up is happening, I just... I just don't know what." He still didn't respond. I probably deserved that. "I'm calling it, Chuck. We're bugging out, I don't care if they bust me down for it. We're getting the others and we're getting out of here." I looked up at that. I wanted to yell when my eyes landed on Chuck, but my throat locked up and the sound barely made it out of my mouth. Wilkins was still leaning against the control panel. He didn't have much choice; he'd been tied there. His helmet sat on a console a few feet away. He took it off sometimes when he worked. His wrists had been tied to the panel with loops of electrical wire. Someone had clawed his eyes out with their fingers. Red warning lights were flashing from the readouts. His rosary was still looped around his left wrist. Blood ran down his arm and dripped off the beads with a soft *tap... tap... tap...* I stumbled back, out of the compartment, back into the passageway. I ran down the corridor blindly, not caring where I went as long as it wasn't into that room with the Wilkins and his empty eye sockets. I saw Wilkins leering at me, in the empty doorways and down the branching halls.

I swung around the corner into the ladder well, and I could see amber light glinting off the metal in front of me. I hauled myself up the stairs using my arms as much as my legs. I slammed open the door to the main deck and rushed through, then I was falling, falling, until my back slammed into the deck with a thunderous crash. I groaned and hauled myself to my feet. I was in the ready room, where we had first boarded the ship. I spun around, trying to get my bearings.

My head was still pounding, like someone was hammering tent stakes into my skull through my temples. I saw the airlock and I stumbled towards it. I fairly collapsed against the control panel when I reached it. I punched the equalize button and slumped there, panting, waiting for the door to unlock. I thought my hear might stop when my comm came to life with a squeal. I couldn't hear anything at first, just static and squeals. After a moment I could make out words under the garbled noise. They were faint, pleading, and laced with pain.

"Harper... Please..." It was Cobb's voice. I squeezed my eyes shut. They burned.

164

"Harper... Stuck... Please... Bridge..."

I sobbed. Then I screamed and punched the airlock door. The light above it turned green and there was a pleasant *ding!* to alert me that the pressure had equalized with the ready room. I shoved off the door and stomped across the compartment, back to the ladder. The bridge was on the next level up from the ready room. I climbed the stairs shakily. My breathing was erratic. They told us in boarding school to breath in four seconds, hold four seconds, out four seconds, hold four seconds to control anxiety, but I couldn't get the pattern to stick.

My head was splitting in half, and I had to stumble down the passageway with one hand on the bulkhead. The exoskeleton left a trail of scratches and gouges all the way down the metal surface. There were no intersecting passageways, but every door in the hall was open. I saw sunset- colored light emanating from one, but it was dark and empty when I passed it. I heard a *snap* from another and dozens of small black beads skittered out of the doorway. I stumbled away from them, and a hand landed on my shoulder, but there was nothing behind me when I turned. I heard whispering from all around and I couldn't *find* anything. I backed away, lamp flashing here and there. There I saw Wilkins, but he was gone when I swept the lamp back to the same spot. There was the outline of an ovoid rock, light emanating from the far side. Something touched my back and I spun, lashing out with the fury of a terrified man.

My suit's gauntlet slammed into the bridge hatch hard enough that it left a dent as deep as my hand was wide. The whispering was rushing towards my back, and I had to get away. I mashed the door control and threw myself inside. I slammed the door shut and put a rivet through the controls.

"*James,*" someone whispered in my left ear. I jerked away but there was nobody There. My light flashed around the compartment and I saw a figure in the pilot's seat. I grabbed the chair and spun it around roughly. The body smiled up at me beatifically, like the man had died right after being granted ultimate enlightenment. It was an expression of rapture marred only by his empty eye sockets. And the blood covering his arms from the broken and missing fingernails all the way to the elbows.

There was nobody else on the bridge. An alarm bleated from the console, and my gaze dropped to the display panel. Norm and the shuttle were gone. That was the first thing I noticed. The second was that the console was blaring a collision warning. I looked out the view screen and swallowed. *Maneki-neko* hurtling toward an asteroid three times her size. The ship was too small to have a lifeboat. I looked at the collision alarm. I had less than two minutes. I couldn't make it all the way to the airlock in time. Not with the door controls fried. I would have to cut my way out.

Cut my way out, I thought desperately. I spun back to the viewscreen. I flexed the fingers on my right hand in a control pattern and a circular saw slid into place with a *shunk-chunk*. It screamed to life with a whine and I plunged it into the view screen. I could see the asteroid in the distance. It was a speck to the naked eye, but things move fast in space and it would look a whole lot bigger very soon. The saw shrieked as it cut through the carbon matrix of the viewscreen. As soon as it punched through the carbon, air began rushing through the thin gap.

There was an explosive *crack* and something slapped my head to the side. I shook my head--aggravating my headache--and stared at my arm. The blade had shattered. I barked out a single hysterical laugh at that. I ejected the remains of the blade. My fingers moved in a practiced pattern and the reciprocating saw slid into place. I shoved the blade through the half-finished cut from the circular saw and flicked the power. It shuddered into life with tooth-rattling oscillations, chewing through the carbon matrix with graceless ease.

The asteroid was now the size of a coin in the distance, and I could *see* the speed of our approach in how rapidly it seemed to be growing. I tried to keep my eyes off it and on my cut. Staring at the rock wouldn't do me any good. I finished the second cut and started the third in my crude triangle. I was a quarter of the way there. The asteroid was the size of a baseball. Halfway there, a soccer ball. Three quarters of the way there. The rock took up half of the view screen. I could hear whispered laughter all around me.

I punched the viewscreen once, twice, it blew out on the third strike and I clambered through. Then hands grabbed the plates of my exoskeleton and I stopped short. I screamed in desperation. I was now exposed, stuck in the viewport like some demented figurehead as the *Maneki-neko* rushed towards oblivion. I struggled fruitlessly, and I could see amber light shining from the cockpit behind me. My right hand stretched in front of me, straining to grab hold of something, anything that could heave me out of the death trap surrounding me.

My eyes landed on it, and I remembered a key feature of the suit. I moved my fingers, activating one final control, and Ceecee, my trusty combination of toolbox and suit of armor, *blew* open. The front of the suit violently swung apart like a clamshell as did the limbs. I heaved out of the suit and I swore I could feel fingers brush my ankle as I kicked out and away from the doomed *Maneki-neko*. I kicked off the line of travel as hard as I could, trying to clear the asteroid. It couldn't have been more than a kilometer in diameter, but in that moment it looked every bit as big as the planet I'd grown up on. I made it, barely. I was only a couple hundred meters away from the rock when I hurtled past. I kept going.

It took them a little over two days to track down my emergency beacon and pull me in. Fifty-three hours of drifting with no control and no ability to to anything besides relive the events of the *Maneki-neko*. When they hauled me in, they said I was lucky to come back. I gave them enough of the truth, but it never went anywhere. I was the lone survivor of a mission that quickly became a textbook example of just how wrong things can go.

The official story was that the ship had been irreparably damaged in the crew's desperate Hail Mary jump, and that any survivors--and my team--had been killed by a malfunction of the drive control, which lead to impact with a wandering asteroid. A freak accident; nothing anyone could have done about it. They chalked my story up to post-traumatic stress disorder combined with hypoxia, malnutrition, and some good old fashioned survivor's guilt. They took me out of the fleet after that and assigned me to a nice job on a station. I didn't resent it. I wasn't what I was and the brass were trying to look out for me. I left not long after. I needed answers to questions no one else was willing to ask.

Chapter Seventeen

I blinked and found myself back in my body. My throat was raw, my eyes were strained, and my face felt wet. There was blood drifting around the inside of my helmet, I figured it was from my eyes and nose because I could feel a crust of dried blood in both places. My throat felt raw, and I dully remembered screaming for what felt like a very long time. Or maybe trying not to scream.

I think it took me a very long time to assemble a train of thought again, to remember who and where I was, and what I was trying to do. I realized that I had given myself a very slight spin when I kicked off of the cryopod. That was what had saved me. My rotation had eventually taken my line of sight away from the thing they were stretching across the span of the hold.

Get away.

I thought about the moment when my spin would bring that thing back into my field of vision again and I twitched.

Not again. The thought was desperate.

My hands shook as I searched my body for something, anything, that could help me here. I didn't have much. I was down to the very last few feet of fry-wire, a crowbar that was no use at the moment, and my a-knife. The chem lamp was getting dimmer all the time, and although my CO_2 scrubbers and O_2 tanks were good, they wouldn't last forever. I needed something, anything, to get me away from that monstrosity. I scanned the darkness around me for anything that might possibly be useful and stretched my arms out to their full length to take advantage of the conservation of momentum and slow my spin.

There was nothing, out there in the perfect darkness. Nothing of use. My injuries throbbed, and had found a new ally in the blazing migraine I had picked up at some point during... during some things I would rather not think about. I let out a hoarse growl of frustration. I wondered in that moment if God had some personal problem with me in particular. So I took a deep breath, closed my eyes. and I lit my candles again. One by one, I brought up the little tricks of imagination that let me shut away all the things that wouldn't help me accomplish my mission: fear, blue candle. Pain, red candle. Weariness, grey candle. Whatever had just happened to me... Black candle. Black flame. It was a new one, a new image. It was needed. When I opened my eyes, I was in control again. I was focused, alert. All those things were still there, the candles were just mind tricks to help me ignore things that were unproductive. I was still battered, bloody, tired, angry, and afraid. But I was calling the shots again and that would do.

Think, James. There's an answer here, so stop fucking around and find it.

172

That was more like it. I was recovering a useable frame of mind. I ran through my gear again and I found something I had passed over the first time that completely changed my perspective: a canister of water. The twin to the one I had used to improvise a grenade in the engineering bay. I thought I could use this one in a similar way, for a very different end. What I needed was a way to get away from that *thing* as fast as possible, and I believed I had thought of one. I carefully pulled a length of fry wire from my belt, only about six inches or so. I didn't need much.

Next I whipped out my a-knife and positioned it just below the valve of the water canister in a bizarre parody of the tradition people still kept with bottles of champagne. Then I had to do the hardest thing I'd ever done. I had to wait. For this to work, I had to be facing the Glyph. I tried very hard not to think about that, and the black flame on that black candle wavered whenever I felt the blood leaking from my eyes and nose. My hands shook a little.

Easy, Jim. Just take it easy. It's a simple plan, you just have to do it.

I shuddered occasionally, and I eventually brought my arms in to touch my sides to speed up the spin. The sooner I got this done, the sooner I could get away from this miserable fucking scow. I clenched my teeth and counted heartbeats until I saw red light creeping into my peripheral vision. I squeezed my eyes shut through the blood and sweat and waited until I could feel the light covering my field of vision. Then I moved. My right hand sliced the top of the water canister while my left braced it against my stomach, near my navel. I flicked my a-knife closed and stuffed it

173

into its sheath. Then I lit the fuse on the fry wire and jammed it into the open neck of the canister.

There was a split-second delay, and then the canister slammed into my stomach hard enough to activate my suit's shock absorption layer, the belly of the suit stiffening to protect me from the blunt impact. *Protected* doesn't mean *comfortable* though, ask anyone who's been shot while wearing armor. The impact forced my eyes open and for a split second, before the cloud of water vapor from my improvised rocket obscured it and I was shoved away at velocity, I saw the Glyph.

My improvised rocket engine didn't last long; that was fine. You don't need much when there's no drag to fight. The flip side was that once I got moving, there was nothing to slow me back down. Unless I hit something. Best not to think about that. All I had to do was wait out the ride and try to think of a way to stick the landing. That would be easier said than done but after I shook the sight of the—after I relit the black candle, I had most of my remaining wits about me. How much that meant I didn't know, but it beat being mind-locked by whatever the hell that thing was. I hurtled through the empty bay like a forlorn comet traversing the infinite dark between the stars, blissfully freed from the awful awareness of the nightmare construction in the center of the hold for a brief moment. I savored that fact for a moment, ignoring the dread lingering in my gut.

Focus, James.

I craned my neck around, searching for something to break the darkness. I had no frame of reference so I didn't feel like I was moving after the initial shove from the improvised rocket I had made. With no frame of reference and a constant velocity, it felt as though I were simply floating weightlessly. I had learned the dangers of that when I slammed into that cryopod not long ago. Just because you don't feel like you're moving, doesn't mean that you aren't. I tried to turn myself around so I was facing in the direction of my travel through the careful manipulation of my arms and legs, but I couldn't tell if I was actually accomplishing anything. Something flashed by me, left to right, and I realized I had spun perpendicular to my line of travel, so I was hurtling towards my left, subjectively speaking.

My next problem was how to decelerate without turning into a stain against the hull. Judging by the relative speed of the object I had just passed, I reasoned that I was moving fast enough to hurt quite a bit when I hit. The problem was, there was no way for me to decelerate. I had no more water. Almost no fry-wire. No ammo left for my pistol. Nothing much left to work with. I tried to spin a bit more with my limbs, and I thought I got myself closer to actually my direction of travel, but I couldn't really be sure.

I ran through options in my head, as more pieces of debris started to zip by me. Or maybe I was zipping by them. I still had no way to tell. It may be that I was moving at a relatively slow pace and the pieces of flotsam in the hull were flying by at incredible speed, or it may be that they were actually moving in the same direction as me and I was simply moving so much faster than them that the seemed to be whizzing by like bullets. I wouldn't know until the hull of *Alea* came back into view and I had a frame of reference. At this point that was the most dangerous possibility to me: that I would kill myself colliding with the increasingly dense debris or with the hull of the ship.

I passed dozens of objects the size of my two hands together, and I realized I was passing through a cluster of the small monstrosities I had encountered in the engine room. That didn't tell me much. I didn't know how long I had been under the influence of the glyph in the hold. They could have drifted all the way to the far end by now, for all I knew.

Nothing for it, I thought, *I'll just have to try to roll with the landing.*

Without my suit, it would be suicide. At the speed I was moving, I would pancake like someone trying to *roll with the landing* of a sixty-foot jump. But my suit was designed to stiffen under impact. It was the same technology that had let me survive my tumble down the lift shaft, and it should serve me well here, if I applied it properly. At least, that was what I told myself. There may or may not have been an element of desperation present in my thinking at that point, but I was determined to see this through and I didn't have a huge number of options available to me.

If I managed to get the suit to take the brunt of the force and shed the rest with the roll, there was a decent chance that I would be able to evade another injury. That was crucial. I couldn't afford any more injures at this point. I was already too badly hurt to be much good in a fight. Something glinted ahead of me, and my heart started racing. The good news was that I could see the monorail. The bad news was that I could also see the end of the hold and empty space, and it wasn't clear which I was going to reach first.

Chapter Eighteen

I had two problems. The first was simple: I was going too fast. In the grand scheme of things, on the scale of objects moving through space, I was barely moving at all. But on the scale of human reaction times and fatal deceleration, I was moving too fast. There wasn't anything I could do about that one. The second problem was that I was moving at an oblique angle to the hull of the ship and the mono rail. not quite straight out the back of the hull but the angle was shallow enough that I would only have a few meters to brake against the hull before I drifted out of *Alea's* hold entirely. That was a death sentence. I was pretty sure I had already used my one miracle rescue after the *Maneki-neko.* There were no patrol boats out this far. If I left this hold, I was a dead man. End of story. I had no idea how I had wound up on the wrong side of the web, but at that point it was pointless to wonder.

I cast about for options. I had a small crowbar, my knife, and a pistol with no ammunition. It was more than nothing, but not by much. The hull flashed by beneath me rapidly, but it grew closer only gradually. I could see the ragged edge of the hull ahead. The meter-thick metal had been left in a jagged edge. Wires, conduits, and a length of the monorail extended beyond the tear, stretching out towards the distant stars. My eyes were drawn to that emptiness. My stomach felt like it was filled with lead. I couldn't help but remember the long hours of drifting helplessly, all those years ago. I clenched my jaw and forced my eyes to stay on the narrow strip of metal near the edge of the tear. I would have less than twenty meters to stop myself without killing myself or drifting into interstellar space. I didn't have time to formulate an actual plan before I hit.

I did the best I could. I pulled my crowbar out of my bag and swung my arm slightly. That set my body spinning, very slowly. I craned my neck to check my timing. Twenty meters. Ten meters. Five. I tucked my chin to my chest and threw out the arm with the crowbar. My only good arm at that point. That served to slow my spin and get the crowbar in position, *hopefully*, to snag a joint or cable on the hull and slow me down. I was now approaching the hull back first.

There was a drawn-out moment of silence after I lost sight of the hull. Then I *slammed* into the metal violently. The breath left my lungs and something yanked viciously at the crowbar. For half a second, I thought the plan had worked perfectly. Then the tension in my arm let go suddenly, and I bounced. I was drifting away from the hull now, and I had started an end over end spin. It looked like the metal plates were coming at me straight on and rushing over my head. I something was snagged on the crowbar and I felt a light impact on my back. I snatched wildly with my other hand, the bad one. My fingers closed around a slim shape, and then the arm was torn nearly out if its socket again.

I swung like a rock on a string and slammed into the hull. I still didn't stop moving. My new position was like sliding down a cliff on my belly. There were periodic jerks on my left arms, and I could feel myself losing velocity with each one. Just not fast enough. I craned my neck and looked at my lifeline, my only connection to the ship and life. It was a wire no bigger around than a pencil. I couldn't conceive what a wire that small was even doing in the hold of a ship like *Alea*. I looked down between my boots just in time to see them slide over the edge of the ragged metal. My body followed, and then I was *outside*. The last place any space farer ever wants to find himself. I looked over my head just in time to see the wire I'd been tearing out of its mounts reach the edge and rip free.

My stomach dropped all the way back to the ground on the last planet I'd been on.

No, I thought eloquently.

I was drifting. I could see *Alea* slowly pulling away from me. Amber lights glinted in the depths of the hold. I could faintly see stars twinkling in the vast darkness around me. I was a dead man.

Chapter Nineteen

The wire drifted out from my hand like a string drifting on a current. I wasn't sure why I was still holding it. Miraculously, I had retained the crowbar in my other hand. I looked at the two items dumbly for a moment, and then the circuit closed and a jolt of electricity ran through my body. I twitched with eagerness and then forced myself back to stillness. Even that motion had affected my drift a bit. I very, very slowly brought the two items together. It had never occurred to me before that the crowbar was almost the same shape as an old school fishhook. I wound the wire carefully into a knot fisherman had probably been using for millennia. It took several nerve-wracking minutes of slow work, steadily watching the edge of the ship drift further and further away. But as I tightened the final loop of the knot, I felt a thrill of excitement.

Very slowly, I moved my head up and scanned the ragged edge of the hold. Now I just needed a target. I carefully spooled the line up in my bad hand. My good hand clenched the makeshift grappling hook. I could see a few likely targets, but I didn't have enough wire to reach them. The ship was already too far away. I strained my eyes, looking first left, then right.

There.

There was something to my right, at the very edge of my peripheral vision. I twisted my head at a glacial pace. The strand of monorail I had seen earlier stuck out from the rest of the jagged hull like a quay jutting out into the infinite ocean of space. Massive columns suspended it fifteen meters out from the surface of the hull. It was one of those columns that had caught my eye. I eyed the distance. I thought I could make it. The risk was that any missed throw would accelerate me away from *Alea* and make subsequent throws less likely to succeed.

I licked my lips, judged the distance, and swung the hook out in a gentle arc. There was no reason to muscle it, that would only make the counter rotation worse. The little piece of metal, my improvised grapple, swung out past the column. The wire swept along behind it, tracing the radius of its arc. I saw the wire wrap around the metal column, felt it grab a bit, but I waited. The crowbar came around the other side of the column, slowly wrapping the wire around the tree sized beam.

I waited until it had reached the very end of the line, just before it would rebound and begin to unwind itself, the I swung my boots forward and *heaved.* The wraps around the metal stanchion tightened down. The mass of the crowbar helped me there. It would have to decelerate, stop, and then accelerate in the other direction to unwrap the wire from the post. It held. I flew towards the beam, faster than was actually wise, but I caught the impact primarily on my good leg. I felt my mag boots adhere to the surface and I started laughing. I looked down over my shoulder like a rappeler looking down the world's highest face. Stars were below me. I gathered up the improvised grappling hook and made my way up, onto the surface of the monorail. In

184

spite of everything, I couldn't help but smile. At least until the glimmer of orange light in the hold caught my eye, and I remembered that I very badly needed to be on the other side of that.

Chapter Twenty

The monorail was an I-shaped metal structure roughly eight feet wide and fifteen high. It made for a strange road, lit as it was by the bloody light of my lamp. I pulled myself doggedly down it, one laborious step at a time. The crowbar was back in my bag. The wire wouldn't fit, so I clutched it in one hand. "Walking" with mag boots in zero gravity bears little resemblance to walking, but my bad leg didn't appreciate the distinction. I kept my eyes nailed to the smooth metal in front of my boots. I did not look up. Not when I could help it. The first kilometer or so was eerily calm. My lamp didn't reach all the way down to the hull of the ship, and the monorail had the appearance of a path that rose out of pitch blackness as I approached, then sank back to nothingness as I passed.

Occasionally I passed a floating chunk of debris or a cargo pod. It was surreal passing house-sized chunks of metal simply floating in the air, to my perspective. I reflected that it was odd that I found that odd, given the things I had seen in the recent past, but some things our brains just don't really get, and zero gravity is one of them.

After maybe a kilometer and a half, I started to see the most distant strings of the web. The light seemed to slither over them, but from a distance they could almost be suspension cables for a bridge or anchor cables for a transmitter tower. They grew gradually more numerous as I walked. Before long, they crossed over head and on every side at all angles. I felt like a fly trying to sneak through the web of a particularly malevolent spider. I kept my eyes off the long strands as much as I could.

Sometimes they were anchored to the monorail though, and I would have to walk down on the side of the rail to go around them. I never made the mistake of looking directly at any of them, but I could see a great many limbs twisted together in my peripheral vision. I thought I could hear a familiar susurrus from some of them when I got too close. I seriously contemplated dropping all the way down to the hull after I noticed that, but the monorail would mean the shortest route back to *Erebus*.

Something like a klick after I had seen the first threads, they had become so dense that I was constantly weaving around them. Every now and again I would sense movement at the edge of my vision, and I recalled the creatures I had seen scuttling about the web from afar. The fact that I had seen them from as far away as I had was not comforting. That meant they were big. Maybe not as big as the limb-worm from the ship's interior, but big enough.

The movement wasn't the worst part of the trip. I started seeing things before long. I would catch a glimpse of Wilkins drifting by, or stuck in one of the webs. I saw Cobb lurking behind drifting flotsam. And the whispering drowned out everything else. It didn't sound any louder, but I had tried to talk to myself to cover over the noise and I couldn't hear myself talk. My legs were shaky, and I was losing time. I would come to fifty feet down the track with no memory of having walked the distance. The strands now looked like a parody of a forest.

Trunks made of trunks and limbs made of limbs, I thought with a sort of hysterical humor.

I weaved through a cluster of strands. I couldn't help but notice that one of the arms in the nearest still had nail polish on the fingernails. I shook my head and forced my eyes forward. At first, I wasn't sure what I was seeing. I could see a strange, round object on the track ahead of me. It was translucent and thing, and it looked like things pressed against it from the inside periodically. Now a hand, now a face, now the profile of a feminine leg. I swallowed bile. Something moved ahead of the orb and it shifted over, climbing up the strands and repositioning. The image resolved and I put together what I was looking at. I wish I hadn't.

In form, it was like a tick combined with a spider. One of those spiders with fat, bulbous abdomens and long, spindly legs. The "abdomen" was the sac I had seen first. It was distended like a tick that had gorged itself on blood. The limbs were long twists of muscle and bone, and there were too many of them. It turned to adjust something, and I had the misfortune to see its head. A cluster of messy skulls with glyphs where the eyes should be, surmounted three sets of arms. The arms never stopped moving. Stroking and caressing and patting the webs with delicate care. A shudder passed through the thing and its flesh-sac quivered. It contracted, and limbs slid out of the mouth covered in pinkish mucus. The hands of the mandibles lovingly placed the

189

mismatched parts, guiding them with precision. My stomach heaved, and I very nearly vomited in my helmet. I tore my eyes away, and they landed on something I had missed when my gaze was locked on the weaver. A hulking shape straddled the monorail, enshrouded in flesh-webs. A boxy shape with two prongs standing up from the top.

The monorail car.

My eyes flicked to the spider. It hung over the track maybe five meters. It was bust building another strand of the web. My eyes went back to the car. The hatch into the cargo compartment still seemed to be clear. It sat maybe ten feet above the track. I swallowed. Then I took the first step. I glanced up at the spider. It hadn't moved. I slid my way slowly forward. The monster was still busy with its section of the web. I felt like my body was going to be ripped into pieces from the tension. I glanced up at the halfway mark. It hadn't moved. Three quarters and it had shifted to a slightly different part of the web, further from the car. I was almost to the car.

The next time I looked up. It was gone. I spun around and the building-sized monster was within five feet and coming fast. I cried out and launched myself backwards. The mandible-arms swung through vacuum where I had been. I heaved myself up to the hatch with desperate strength and ripped it open. The inertia swung me around, and my back slammed into the side of the car. It saved my life. The monstrous face slammed into the spot I had occupied a half second before and pulled back. I seized the opportunity to heave myself through the hatch. I flew to the far door and grabbed the lever, and something grabbed my ankle and *pulled*. My knife was in my hand before I consciously thought of needing it and I swept it through the mandible-arm that had seized my calf. It parted below the elbow and the forearm began to drift lazily. I noticed a gold watch on the wrist before I hauled myself through the inner hatch and slammed the door.

Chapter Twenty-One

I stood there with my chest heaving and my heart pounding for a moment before I looked around. I was standing in the crew cabin. The bulkheads to either side of me had a three high set of bunks apiece. Ahead was a small lounge with a card table next to the ladder up to the cockpit, and beyond that an airlock which mirrored the one by which I had entered. On the right bulkhead was a ladder leading up to the cockpit, painted in the universal caution pattern of black and yellow stripes. On the left bulkhead was a door marked **Head**. That made sense. When loading or unloading cargo, these derricks wouldn't stop moving for days at a time.

There would probably be half a dozen men per rig whose sole job in that period was to pick and pull cargo, or else load it into the stacks of *Alea's* gluttonous belly. It was obvious that the three corpses drifting through the small living area had stayed out here deliberately. Food containers and ration packs drifted amongst the frozen corpses. They had probably planned to wait out the chaos in the relative safety of this pod, then return to the crew decks once the crisis had passed.

But it never did pass, did it?

It was sobering to see these men and consider their final days, most likely listening to the carnage happening just a few kilometers away over the internal communications system. There must have been debates about whether to go forward and pitch in with one side or the other. Whether to seize the engines perhaps. None of if happened. These men had likely starved to death, or died of dehydration. Maybe they killed each other in disputes. And the real bitch of it was, *they were the lucky ones.* They were the only ones who had managed to just *die,* without being corrupted into something else. I barked out a harsh laugh, thinking of Isaac Bly and his deal with the devil to secure a clean death.

I guess nobody had a good way out of this nightmare, I though soberly.

The car rang like a bell and I jumped out of my skin. It rocked from side to side, and if there had been any atmosphere out there to conduct sound, I was sure I would have heard a roar. I scrambled across the compartment and hauled myself up the ladder to the cockpit. The cockpit was a geodesic dome of what was probably carbon matrix with the pilot's chair in the center, just behind me as I clambered out of the crew compartment. The chair could face fore or aft if the car was carrying people or supplies to or from the engines at the rear of the ship, or lay back and face inboard when the car was needed to move cargo. The Car rattled again and I looked to the rear of the compartment. I could see the distended sac of the spider rippling as the head and forelimbs savagely attacked the hatch and the rear of the monorail car. I jumped into the pilot's seat and scanned the controls. They were blissfully simple, as the controls for heavy machinery tend to

194

be. I grabbed the stick and hit the primary power. I hoped furiously for several seconds. Nothing happened. I cursed. The spider slammed the car again, harder.

Then a light blinked on. Then another. The car rumbles as power surged through it. The stick came to life in my hand, and I *slammed* it to my left, desperate to be moving forward again. The car started left, then shuddered to a stop. For the first time I looked out the viewing dome.

The web.

Strands of flesh were anchored to the car on almost every surface, and they led my eyes up, into the heart of... I coughed, and blood splattered the inside of my helmet. I yanked my eyes off the web and threw the stick to my right. The tension on the car relaxed and then it accelerated aft. I felt a *whump* as the massive block of metal hit the spider. strands of the web parted. Vicious satisfaction surged up in me, and I switched direction again. The lurched forward, then paused, straining. I raked the controls until I found the one I needed. I threw the switch that engaged the car's cargo handling mode. I could feel the torque increase. The spider latched onto the rear of the car with its forelimbs. The web strained, parted, and the car *flew* down the track, plowing through the web without issue now that it had some inertia behind it. When I looked back, I saw that the two forelimbs of the spider were still attached, and I had to laugh.

...

Zipping up the track in the car was the closest thing to relaxation I'd had since I accepted this job a few days ago. Naturally then, it wasn't meant to last. The pilot's chair had rotated ninety degrees to face the direction of travel when I had selected the forward dock as the destination. I didn't have much control while the unit was docked to the sled--I could pretty much speed up, slow down, and perform rudimentary actions with the manipulators. Thankfully, I didn't need much control: I just needed to get back to engineering. According to the system diagram on the console, this monorail was on the port side, second from the bottom. That wasn't actually a bad place to be. It would put me within a few hundred meters of the hole I had blown into engineering a short while ago, and while there was a route to get there from the very lowest levels where this car docked, I liked a short spacewalk better than trying to clear cramped corridors with nothing but my and a-knife and moxie. I was trying to plan for my route to the reactor when an alarm started blaring at me. My gaze flicked down to the console readout:

OBSTRUCTION ON TRACK: ENGAGE BRAKES

I looked out the forward section of the track just as the forward floodlights illuminated the obstruction rapidly closing the distance: A long, worm like object. Flesh colored, and writhing.

"Motherfu--"

Impact.

196

Chapter Twenty-Two

Some assholes just can't take a damn hint. The impact with the mass of flesh slammed me into the control console as the entire assembly decelerated. The front of the thing snaked through the manipulator arms and slammed into the crash cage around the cockpit dome. Arms flailed through the gaps in the cage and slammed into the transparent facets with a surprising amount of force, like the world's most malevolent hailstorm:

thunk, thunk, thunk,crack!

My eyes snapped to the crack that had just appeared on the dome.

Ok, not *carbon matrix then, just glass.*

My appreciation for the engineering of the monorail dropped immensely. After the first crack appeared, more followed. I stole a glance at the tram map. we were roughly halfway back to the forward portion of the ship and engineering. There was a quick *crack, crack, crack,* then a roar as the glass finally hit its failure point and blew out from the internal air pressure. The hand sized shards of glass *shredded* the limbs of the beast nearest the dome, shearing them off to spin through the void. I felt vindictive satisfaction at that. The downside to the loss of the glass was that there was no real barrier between me and the monster now. It began feeding its mass of limbs through the gaps in the crash cage, simply sliding around the bars and into my last little sanctuary. My heart rate spiked. I couldn't hold the tram. An idea occurred to me in that moment:

Maybe I don't have to.

I wrapped my right hand around the throttle lever, my left around a different control, and looked that freak right in the asshole it used for a face.

"You want it, fucker? You got it."

I slammed the throttle forward, all the way to the stop. The acceleration instantly slammed me back into the seat, and made the rest of the Big One's considerable mass pile up at the front of the car. Right between the jaws of the manipulator arm. I crushed the control in my left hand, and the jaws of the manipulator sprang shut. I swear I felt the crunch through the soles of my boots as the huge mass of limbs was crumpled like a ball of foil. I flicked open my a-knife and sheared off the throttle and brake levers--it seemed wise given the number of hands this thing had. I slapped the release for the restraints and hauled myself out of the pilot's seat. I had to move quickly, or I would get caught in my own trap. I pulled myself to the edge of the dais, shoulder screaming, and got a hand on the safety railing around the ladder to the lower deck. However the huge creature perceived the world, it clearly saw that I was up to something. Limbs started dropping off it and wriggling towards me over the deck, flopping spasmodically across the alloy plates.

198

That's a new one, I thought sourly. I didn't let it slow me down though. I swung around the safety rail and dropped into the ladder well, sliding to the bottom as part of the same motion. My boots hit the deck--pain lanced up from my ankle--and I took a single limping step before something slapped me across the shoulders. I spun in a circle and threw off an arm. It glowed with a glyph in the center of a ragged palm, and when it impacted one of the bulkheads the palm slapped against the panel, launching it back towards me. There was almost something comedic about it, but I had already seen how effective a horde of small threats could be, so I wasn't about to take any chances. I flicked out my knife in a flash and slashed through the glyph on the palm with no resistance. I had a half second to process what had just happened, and then a dozen more launched themselves down the ladder well at me.

Fuck this noise.

I dashed to the back of the car and grabbed the last thing I needed for the rest of this plan. I felt a few more limbs slap the back of my suit, a few even got a painfully tight grip on my limbs, but I had bigger concerns. I sprinted, or as close to a sprint as I could still manage, to the rear airlock and threw it open, dragging my haul from the bunk along with me. I bounded across the short space and threw open the secondary door. Something in my brain expected the rush of wind, but there was no atmosphere outside, so there was simply nothingness as I swung out the doorway. I planted my boots on the side of the car and walked *up*, relative to the deck of the car, as quickly as I could manage. My heart was pounding.

Any second now...

I crested the top of the car and took a step between the jaws of the manipulator on this side. I was looking down the car, through the shattered cockpit dome and the crash cage. Right at the writhing mass of flesh that was my enemy. I swear it saw me, in that last second. It seemed like the whole thing went still. I did the only thing that came to mind: I flipped it off.

"Have a nice trip, asshole," I said. Then I pushed off with my legs as hard as I could, while simultaneously deactivating my mag boots. I grunted a bit under the strain of launching both myself and my little souvenir, but I managed.

My boots left the car, and I drifted up at what felt like a sedate pace. If the car had felt like being at the bottom of the ocean, then the jump felt like ascending from the dive. I saw the limbs of the creature flailing in a universal sign of outrage as it tried to disentangle itself from the crushing grip of the manipulator claw. The car was still accelerating. As it pulled ahead, I looked beyond it and saw the lights at the front of the car illuminate the rapidly approaching docking station. At the last second, the monster might have tried to escape, but it was far too late:

The car slammed into the wall of metal at the front of the hold at something very close to its maximum speed, and just... Didn't stop. The mass of metal plowed through the bulkhead and didn't appear to slow down. A shower of sparks and small explosions sparked around the perimeter of the breach; batteries or fuel cells from the auxiliary power system most likely. It vanished into *Alea's* superstructure like a bullet into a tree stump. There was a half second of stillness, and then a blast blossomed from the hole. From what I could remember of the schematics, it seemed likely it had struck a fuel tank or pump room. I flipped off the empty, cavernous space one more time.

"End of the line, asshole," I said wearily.

Chapter Twenty-Three

I had dealt with the biggest threat of which I was aware, but I wasn't out of the woods yet. I still had to make sure I didn't splat myself against the hull too. When I jumped *up* from the roof of the car, what I was really doing was jumping *inboard*, towards *Alea's* center line. That and the fact that I had been moving just as fast as the tram car when I jumped meant my trajectory was a diagonal line from where I departed the car to the approximate center of the bulkhead which was the end of the hold. That was good; it should put me reasonably close to the hole I had blown out into the hold a few...

Hours? Minutes?

...Earlier. The hole I had made earlier, before I got... Distracted. The problem was that I could now tell, by using the hole from the tram as reference, that I was still holding too much speed. With no atmosphere or maneuvering jets to conveniently bleed speed, I needed another way to adjust my velocity. I'd had to think fast when I came up with this plan, and that was where my souvenir came in. On my way off the car, I had grabbed the only thing in the car that had the mass that I needed for my idea to work:

One of the former crew members of the *Alea*.

It didn't exactly sit right with me, using a cadaver as tool like that, but my options were very limited and I was down to a life-or-death wire. I needed something massive enough that it could act as a counterweight to me. I'm not a huge guy, but I had a decent velocity and I had a lot of inertia to offset. So I had grabbed the largest of the three cadavers from where they had all been drifting against the back wall of the car. The guy I had grabbed should be plenty big enough, but I only had one chance, and without a frame of reference at the moment, I couldn't actually tell my own direction of travel. Without that knowledge, this maneuver was just as likely to accelerate me even further and make my landing worse, rather than decelerate me and give me a survivable landing.

I craned my neck and strained my eyes to peer into the darkness, looking for a reference point. For a few moments, moments in which I knew I was hurtling towards a very solid metal wall, without the *authority* of the monorail car, there was nothing. Nothing but darkness. My gaze raked the shadows as I scrabbled for any scrap of information.

There.

A flash. I focused my gaze just to the side of where I thought I had seen the light, the same way you do when you're trying to see a particularly dim star at night. There it was again--the emergency lights must have activated in engineering when I depressurized the space. Another system running on a separate power supply. Whoever was in charge of *Alea's* safety redundancies, they weren't paid nearly enough. I watched for the next flash, and my heart skipped a beat. I was going to over shoot the hole by a fair distance, but it was roughly ahead of me. I had gotten my orientation right when I made the jump from the tram car.

Given the circumstances of my departure, I thought that was pretty good work. I slowly maneuvered the cadaver into position, keeping an eye on the intermittent flashes of light from the approaching gap. What I needed most was to kill as much momentum in the forward direction as I could. The lateral momentum was from my jump alone, and wasn't a primary concern. The velocity I had picked up from the monorail was my main concern. I waited until I thought the distance was about a hundred meters "above" the bulkhead and then kicked off the cadaver with both feet as hard as I could.

Sorry, buddy, was all the apology I could afford to give the poor spacer who'd become my counterweight. I promised myself that if anybody ever used my body for something like this after *I* died, I wouldn't mind a bit. It seemed fair.

I focused. I lost sight of the flashing emergency lights from engineering after I overshot the gap, and I needed all my attention on the limited range of my chem lamp. I'd only have a split second to--

Roll!

I curled my body as the wall came into the short range of my lamp and stiffened my legs. My boots slammed into the hard metal... And my ankle held! I *threw* my weight forward, over my shoulder, and this time I actually managed to roll. It was still a bit of a rough landing, but I managed to get my boots on in time to prevent me from drifting off the surface. Once my feet stuck I pivoted around them and had to brake the rest of my momentum with my good arm, but I had made it successfully. I barked out a single

"*Hah!*" Of triumphant laughter, and punched the void in satisfaction.

That wasn't bad, James... Not bad at all.

It may have been self-congratulatory in the most literal sense possible, but what the hell. I had earned it. I stood slowly so as not to throw myself around in zero-g, and turned around. There, maybe fifty meters away, I could see the emergency lights glinting on the ragged edges of metal around my makeshift exit. I checked my gear, focused myself, and started walking.

...

The flashes of light from engineering meant the opening alternately had the appearance of a pool of complete darkness, and a cliff dropping away into a bottomless chasm of metal. Looking down at the passage, and then back up into the darkness above me, I once again had the surreal impression of being stuck at the bottom of an endlessly dark ocean, one full of predators unseen by human eyes since some dark god molded them out of primordial muck and hid them in the shadowed places of the deep. That thought was far too close to reality for my liking, so I took a breath and swung my good leg over the threshold of the opening for the artificial gravity to catch... and felt nothing. It

206

seemed like the system had failed, at least locally. That would more than likely play against me, since I was even slower in my mag boots than running on my bad leg.

Not like I'm exactly drowning in options here, though...

I swung my good leg down to catch the deck of the bay with my boot. I hauled myself through the opening, stuck my bad leg to the deck, and I was once again standing on the metal floor of what I had come to see as my very own personal hell. I jerked my leg up to take a step—and froze. My chem lamp was dimming all the time, which was concerning given that they were rated for twenty-four hours of useable lighting before they died, but the bloody light of the lamp and the intermittent, too-white flashes of the emergency strobes were enough for me to see I hadn't gotten off quite as free as I thought.

There were still... Pieces spread around the deck like toys left behind after a toddler's tantrum, and some still had glyphs burning on them. They all seemed to be damaged in some way, missing legs or other bits, but there was no clear path to get where I needed to go. The plan from here on out was simple: Get to the reactor, light the fuse, and then wait for a new star to be born and die in the blink of an eye. As plans went I felt that it lacked somewhat in elegance, but it made up for that with thermonuclear annihilation, so it worked out.

I looked at the mess of body parts, servos, and scraps of metal. If these were inert remains of former... Constructs? Then they would've been vented into the bay with the rest of the drones, not laid out like... Like a net. It hit me, and I realized that every

207

piece or part was touching at least one other on the deck. There was no pattern, as such, but all the same I knew exactly where I was: I was standing in the galaxy's biggest spiderweb, and it had been laid out specifically for a fly named Harper. My spine crawled, and I thought to myself that it seemed like my life saved all the real nasty surprises for the final act. I eyed the web of assorted parts on the floor again, and then looked up at the cyclopean machines that filled the space. There was realistically only one way to get into the center of the engine room without touching those things, so I started walking. To my right.

I walked to the edge of the hole I had blasted in the bulkhead what felt like days ago, carefully avoiding the skinless leg and broken strut that had been draped across my path. I only moved far enough to be able to lift up a leg and get my boot onto the bulkhead where it was still solid. It should have been a simple operation, but my bad leg made it a lot more painful than I would have liked. I was glad that I wasn't drifting powerlessly in the hold anymore, but I was under no delusions as to the state of that leg. If I had to move quickly--especially if the artificial gravity came back online--I wasn't going to make it.

After a pained grunt of effort, I was trudging up the bulkhead, which was now the floor to me, and I was treated to the perspective of being at the bottom of the metal chasm I had seen on the way in. It was equally unsettling standing on a surface of blank, polished metal, staring up at the myriad alien forms of the sub-drive, the computers and machines and fabricators and coolant systems that had kept *Alea* running while she made her lonely treks between the stars. I had that deep-sea trench vertigo again, so I focused on the nearest machine, disengaged my mag boots, and jumped. Moving in zero g like that always feels like being in water to me.

A lot of spacers have never been swimming, but I grew up planet side, so I used to swim regularly when I was young. It's been decades now but I still feel like I'm kicking off the bottom of the lake whenever I do a free jump like that, just drifting effortlessly. The presence of a tangible target in front of me and the periodic illumination from the flashing lights made it an entirely different experience to drifting through the cavernous hold a few minutes ago. The strobing lights created the strange impression that I was teleporting through the air in short hops. At this point, the words *slow is smooth, and smooth is fast* were the name of the game. It would be bitter irony to break my neck now. I managed to snag a handhold on the machine, one of the massive pumps necessary for the running of the reactor, and slowed myself to a stop with a grunt of effort.

I pulled myself to the top of the machine, relative to the deck of the space, and looked out across the space. I couldn't see any constructs besides the web in the flashing lights. I knew there would be something though. There would be more to this trap than was apparent on the surface. I peered across the tops of the building sized machines to the reactor. It looked like a straight shot, but there would be a catch somewhere. That being said, I wasn't flush with options. I knew it was a trap, but I also knew that I needed to get to that reactor to prevent the completion of whatever it was they were building in the hold, and the opposition clearly knew it. My clumsy run to the reactor earlier had shown my hand, and they had taken a smart strategy: hunker down and use the reactor as bait. They'd read me. They knew that if I didn't die in the hold, I would come back here. I glanced down at the web.

But why just the deck?

That was the question. If this was a trap, why hadn't they accounted for the lack of gravity?

Unless...

I pictured the tram car slamming into the ship and the blast that followed. It was a distinct possibility that there had still been gravity in the space until I rammed the monorail car into the superstructure at maximum velocity. I may have inadvertently knocked out gravity in engineering in my bid to destroy the monster that had been chasing me since I boarded the vessel. It was plausible, but I doubted that the lack of gravity would be enough to completely invalidate the enemy's plan. There was no way I was about to get sloppy now. With no other options but to continue, though, I simply sized up the gap to the next machine--a massive fabricator, by the look of it--and kicked off.

The silence ate at me. There are few things more stressful than being in the middle of a trap that has yet to spring. The tension and the constant threat of a foe with unknown capabilities grind at your focus. I had to use my candle trick a lot on the solitary flight across the stadium-sized compartment. After ten minutes and at least as many jumps from machine to machine, I caught myself on one of the machines that formed the perimeter of the central "plaza", in whose center the reactor stood dormant:

210

It was a massive geodesic shape like an abstract tree stump, surrounded by catwalks and connected to the rest of the ship by a tangled root system of pipes and cables. Some of those would supply fuel and coolant, others would be delivering the power it generated to hungry systems like the sub-space drive, the six separate monorails, the fabricators and computers, all the myriad systems that greedily drank down energy to keep the ship running when it was operational. I had come up on the reactor from almost directly aft, so the control dais was visible for an instant whenever the strobes blinked on, ahead of me and to the left.

I felt a mix of anticipation and fear, looking at the machine. Anticipation, because this was endgame. The *Alea's* remaining time was down to minutes now. Fear because I didn't have any more time than the ship did. I found it much more difficult to accept my death in practice than in theory. I thought about the thousands of bodies in the hold, stitched together into some unholy *thing.* I still couldn't shake the feeling that there was some level of awareness in the demented flesh puppets. I wish I could say I had a surge of heroic resolve in that moment, maybe raised a fist in righteous fury.

But the truth was, I was tired, and busted up, and I had been fucked up way before I ever set foot on that ship. I didn't really want to die on the *Alea.* I just couldn't walk away. So I set my face and braced myself for action. I ran through the specifications I had hastily memorized after raiding the schematics, made sure that I had everything straight, and nodded to myself.

Go time.

I started maneuvering myself over the equipment to get a good position for a jump. I had barely started moving when I saw movement out of the corner of my eye. I hurriedly activated my boots and anchored myself to the machine, then hunkered down behind a bundle of cable that ran over the top of the servers. I clapped a hand over my lamp and poked my head out to see what had moved, and immediately had to bite back a curse.

And there's the trap, I thought to myself.

Chapter Twenty-Four

It came around the reactor from the far side just as I was pulling myself out of my hiding place. It was hard to make out the exact shape in the brief flashes of light. It seemed to be six or seven meters tall. There was a sort of central mass of something that glistened wetly in the lights, surrounded by a constantly shifting set of limb-like protrusions made up of loose tissue and large electrical cables. The center seemed to swivel almost like an eye, an effect exaggerated by the single huge glyph scrawled across one face of it like an iris. It had an oddly smooth, picky gait, and it took me a moment to realize that it wasn't actually walking. Those strange pseudopods would stretch until they made contact with the continuous "web" of viscera lying on the deck and then fuse with the strand, pull the monstrosity forward, and then detach and shrink back towards the center until their mass was needed for another reaching step.

Although the center bore a passing resemblance to an eye, I very much doubted this thing actually hunted by sight—if it did, then it would have spotted the glow of my lamp before I covered it and I would in all likelihood already be dead. It seemed likely it operated much more like a spider, almost exactly like one in fact: any contact with the web would probably have either trapped me, summoned the nerve center, or both. The image came to mind unbidden of myself frantically trying to get a leg out of the grasp of one of the web strands while the titanic abomination bore down on me with that silent, too smooth gait. I was suddenly very glad I had listened to my paranoia about the mess on the floor.

I watched the thing from the scant cover of my hiding spot for a moment. My only real option was to wait the thing out: I had no ammo left for Jericho, my fry-wire was gone, and I was effectively down two limbs. I wouldn't bet on myself in a fight with a regular human at that moment, much less against a twenty-foot-tall colossus cobbled together from machines and flesh. The only thing that mattered was getting to the reactor controls, so I forced myself to watch and wait.

After a minute or so, it passed out of sight around the edge of the reactor, and I had to guess that it would continue to patrol that same route. It was almost certainly a guard, left here to prevent me from getting to the reactor. I doubted whether the enemy really understood the use of the reactor or what I wanted to achieve with it, but it was clear that they had correctly identified it as one of my goals. Regardless, I had a job to do. After waiting for it to pass out of sight, I swallowed once and moved limbs that felt electric with nerves to clamber over the bundle of cables that I had hidden behind. I braced myself to push off from the side of the server tower towards the reactor. The unfortunate thing about this was that I still had the same problem as I had before: I couldn't afford to move faster than I could reliably brake, or I would risk causing myself further injury or rebounding off into the open space of the engine bay. This meant that I had to deliberately drift at what felt like a snail's pace across twenty meters of completely open space. I would have absolutely no ability whatsoever to change my trajectory or back track. If the Crawler, as I termed it for my own reference, came around the reactor and ran into me before I reached the other side, I would be utterly defenseless. I felt a sick feeling in my stomach at that thought. But sometimes when life deals you a shit hand your best bet is to double down and play. So I jumped.

That drift was among the most nerve-wracking experiences in my life; there was nothing to do but wait and sweat. I had no real capacity to change the outcome if the guard decided to turn around, or speed up, or if I had misjudged and it could in fact see me hanging there like a fool. It brought back memories of the time after the *Maneki-neko*. Sweat broke out on my brow thinking about that.

Calm down, James, I told myself. *Just stay cool.*

Maybe I mistimed the jump. Maybe I just moved too slow. Maybe the guard spider sped up around the other side of the rector or had its own version of instinct. I couldn't tell you. But the walker came back at the worst possible time. Smoothly, silently, it reached and fused and dragged and tore its way around the reactor. I turned my head ever so slightly to look at it and I saw that it was going to collide with me, beyond the shadow of a doubt. There was no way I would miss the drifting mass of limbs that made up its body. Turning my head had given me an ever so slight counter spin, so I stuck out my bad arm to slow the rate of the spin for a moment. Unsure what to do, I watched the creature sliding towards me and got a good look at it for the first time: The center was a glistening mass of what seemed to be...

Grey matter.

It was one huge brain. I didn't like to think about the implications of that. There were perhaps a dozen shorter arms hanging below the body, all ending in ragged talons fashioned out of either metal, or lengths of arm or leg with the exposed bone forming a jagged point. I suppose at a certain point you really have to be flattered at the lengths some things will go to in order to get you dead. As I slowed the spin of my body by extending my arm, by bag shifted across my body and I was struck with a flash of inspiration: My right hand snaked into the bag and grabbed the last thing I had, the last tool up my sleeve. As the walker closed in on me blindly approaching the purpose of its solitary patrol, I gripped the length of metal with nervous fingers, and threw it down between my feet. That direction would be aft, since I was currently parallel to the deck of the space. My trusty little crowbar, one of the last cards I could play, sailed down one of the aisles next to the server stack from which I'd jumped. There was no real way for me to tell if my gambit had been successful until the monster stopped.

It didn't *come* to a stop, it just *stopped*. One second it was moving and then a split second later it was still like statues and rocks are still. Then everything went to hell. It launched itself down the aisle, moving with a speed I would never have thought it possessed, and the floor exploded. Every formerly inert piece of robotics and human cadaver burst into motion and began grasping, reaching, clawing, searching for anything it could grab, or maim. The charnel pit flailed like a macabre version of seaweed in a wild current.

216

I had a brief glimpse of that chaotic scene before I slammed into the reactor with my shoulders and the back of my head. My bad shoulder screamed at me and I grunted the pain out, but then I slapped my right hand down and scrambled for something to hold on to. There was nothing, nothing, There! My hand caught on what felt like a bit of loose wire, and I was able to yank myself to a stop. Or my hand to a stop anyway. My body kept swinging around that focal point until my back swung into the reactor body with a dull thud. My body almost swung away again before I managed to slam my bad leg down onto the reactor and activate my mag boot. Another painful yank, and I was hanging upside down, staring at the veritable sea of the damned reaching up for me.

Flawless execution, James, I though at myself sarcastically.

The carpet of viscera below me was a lot less *below me* than I was comfortable with, and the limbs were still searching for me desperately, but I wasn't in danger of being snagged by any of them at the moment. All the same, I hauled myself into a climbing position against the reactor and moved further away from the mess.

Now for the hard part.

I huffed a laugh, then started climbing down towards the reactor's control panel. Although the "web" of components on the deck was extensive and covered most of the available plating, it rarely rose more than a few feet up the sides of the equipment in the space. The blanket of viscera and flotsam reached maybe five feet up the sides of the reactor vessel. It put me in mind of an old

217

stump in a forest, covered in moss and ferns. This tableau was like the reflection from hell of that idyllic scene. The frantic waving of the biomass had somewhat slowed by the time I traversed the side of the reactor. The ropes of flesh and metal now moved in a kind of sleepy, slow motion, like a toddler reaching out for a favorite blanket, rather than the frantic, starved movements of a few minutes ago. Once again I had the feeling of being a miniscule life form in the tank of a much larger fish as I floated and maneuvered down the alloy cliff that was the reactor vessel. I had come roughly a third of the way around the reactor's circumference from my initial landing spot to get myself in line with the control platform, and it was a bizarre thing to see the waving filaments of the mat below me. My head was constantly swiveling to keep a lookout for the spider; I had no desire to recreate the close encounter I'd just had.

The silence was deafening. With no atmosphere to transmit sounds across open space, the only way for me to pick up vibrations from the outside my suit was through the palms of my suit's gloves or my boots. Occasionally I would feel something—a slight tremor or vibration coming to me from far off. I knew that ordinarily it would just be the ship's hull encountering debris or expanding and contracting due to radiation or a particularly hellish patch of absolute cold. On the *Alea*, I had no such reassurance. There was every chance it was something coming for me or laying the next trap.

Joke's on you, I thought after a particularly strong vibration. My eyes were already on the console.

We're already in the end game, you just can't see it yet.

218

Once I made it to the control panel, then the board would be cleared and there wouldn't be much anybody could do about it. It took some careful, and frankly painful, maneuvering to get myself positioned for my next jump, but I made it. The only thing that really bothered me was that I hadn't seen the big spider again. It wasn't something I really wanted to encounter again, but the fact that it was still out of sight put my hackles up. I had no idea where it was or what it was doing, and there was always the possibility that it had predicted this move and was simply waiting for me to be defenseless again. I paused and took stock of my battered body and tired mind.

Well. More defenseless.

I eyed up the gap to the control console. It was probably less than fifteen meters, but that seemed like a much bigger gap as I stared out over the sea of undulating, grasping lengths of muscle and metal. The control deck was a dais maybe five meters wide, circular and ringed with all the terminals necessary to run and monitor the reactor. When the ship was actually running there probably would have been at least three or four people on watch down here at any given time, adjusting output to demand and performing routine maintenance and diagnostics. The deck of the dais was raised maybe two meters off the deck of the engineering space. It was connected to the body of the reactor by a large conduit about a meter tall by two wide. That would contain all the cables for the myriad controls and sensors needed to keep the machine running and in parameters. The base of the dais would have back up power supply to kick-start the reactor's starter mechanism. The web of the abomination had been...

Grown? Laid?

Up the sides of the dais and along the tops of the terminals, but the center appeared to be mostly clear.

One hell of a target...

I thought as I looked at the uncomfortably small area I would have to land in if I were to avoid getting snagged by the web. My initial jump would have to be perfect. If it wasn't, I would be launching myself directly into the literal jaws of failure, death, and possible reuse as a hideous abomination from some deep level of hell.

No pressure, I thought wryly.

On a good day, rested and at my best, it probably wouldn't have been a hard thing to do. I had not had a good day. I was not rested, and I don't think I've ever been further from my best. My hands were shaking, I was jumpy, and I felt like I hadn't slept in a week. I was wrung out and at the very end of my rope. If I fumbled this jump, it wasn't just that I would die, it was the fact that this ship would eventually get wherever it was going, and its cargo of nightmare monstrosities would more than likely be unleashed on a populated world. I saw the thing in the hold in my mind's eye and my thoughts started to slide into that black hole.

I jerked my focus away from the memory in a panic. That wasn't somewhere I needed to go again. I crouched on the side of the reactor that way for longer than I could really afford to. At the end of the day though, there was only so much calculation to be done. Eventually you just have to tell your body what you need it to do and trust it to figure out the rest. I took one final, deep breath, focused my eyes on the center of the dais, extended my legs, and released my mag boots.

It was another painfully slow trip, but I could afford to miss or rebound even less than I could before. This was the play for all the marbles; it wasn't a time to let my nerves get to me and make me twitchy. My trajectory followed the conduit that led out to the dais, and the limbs, tissues, scraps, and servos of the web were disturbingly close beneath me. Passing over them, lit alternately with the bloody light of my all but spent lamp and the harsh white strobes of the emergency lights, was something akin to flying over one of the levels of hell. It was like looking at the souls of the damned reaching up, trying to drag me down to suffer with them in their angst and self-pity. I was just passing the halfway point of my trip when I saw movement out of the corner of my eye and my heart tried to explode out of my chest. It was the spider, finally back from its long walk just in time to catch a very unfortunate fly.

I couldn't even afford to turn my head too fast because that would set my body spinning and I needed to be correctly oriented to stick my landing. My eyes, however, were straining so hard to see the periphery of my vision that it hurt. I could barely make out the mass of wire and nerve tissue moving smoothly towards the reactor. It seemed to stop again, and I realized it was exactly where I had been when I distracted it. It paused there for a moment, then it began moving again. Directly towards me.

Chapter Twenty-Five

It moved quickly in its strange form of locomotion, bearing down on me as pseudopods reached out, fused with the web, then dwindled and snapped as the main body passed them. It came on like an avalanche of debris from a horrible industrial accident, pieces of metal and droplets of blood drifting off it like shrapnel. My heart was hammering with all its might, so much so that the rhythm of it was pounding in my throat and in my head, and my vocal cords seemed to have been dusted with grit. Not that there was any real use for them at this point, but it would have been nice to at least be able to curse out the monster that was going to murder me. there was nothing to do. Nowhere to go. No way to change my fate. All I could do was watch and yell defiance at the thing as it barreled toward me. As I rasped through a hoarse throat though, something became evident: it wasn't on a line to intercept me. It was going to move past me. I was not, in fact about to be torn limb-from-limb and reassembled into some grotesque caricature of the natural world. Not that second at any rate. I couldn't believe it.

Where?

Where was it going? My eyes flicked around to follow it— and my stomach clenched even harder.

No.

The control deck. It was guarding the control deck. I saw its limbs merge with those ringing the top of the consoles, and the center settled over the platform like a watchtower. I desperately scanned the tangle of limbs now enclosing the consoles like a cage, looking for a gap, a way through. There were a few, but they were closing fast. The same trick rarely works twice, but I had to try something; I was only four or five meters away from the rapidly closing gaps of the thing's limbs. I had no tricks left in my bag. So I pulled the bag itself off my shoulder. Three meters away. I was slightly off, I needed to be more to the left for this to work. The strap of the bag caught on my holster. Two meters. I ripped the bag free and flung it to my right as hard as I could. One meter. I was spinning now, and the gap was too small. It had to be. I watched as a skinless clump of grey matter slid up, closing it more right in front of my face.

Then it froze as my bag landed on the web. I tucked my limbs and slipped through the gap, my visor passing not a centimeter from the limb to which my eyes were glued. I inhaled as much as I could, and I was through. I looked down in time to see the toe of my right boot come within a hair's breadth of touching the limb of the monster. If there had been atmosphere in the space, it would have felt the disturbance in the air and the game would be up. It didn't leave to investigate my decoy. It must be wise to that trick now. But I was in. The limbs continued to accrue matter, and I watched with a sinking feeling as the bars of a prison became the walls of my tomb. I wasn't getting out. There were no gaps bigger than my spread hand left.

I lowered my good leg gently to the deck and engaged the mag boot, careful to avoid any vibration I could. My back was now to the deck because of my spin, and I broke the resulting swing with my good hand, gently. I was staring directly up into the ring of cobbled together pincers, scythes, and talons dangling from the huge mass of nerve tissue that was at the core of this thing. All it would take for the thing to kill me would be for it to slam that forest of sharp implements into the deck of the dais. I wouldn't even have a chance to fight back. There were spaces under some of the consoles where I might be able to hide for a moment, but it wouldn't buy me much in the grand scheme of things. I scanned the consoles, looking for the one I needed.

There.

It was at my nine O'clock. I can't express how unnerving it is to try to sneak past a twenty-foot-tall monster which is quite literally hanging over your head. The only thing I could do was use my imaginary candles to tamp down on the nerves and pay attention to what I was doing. That trick wasn't made for shit like this, but it didn't have to last me much longer. I just needed to be able to input a few commands, and I would win. I glanced at the walls of flesh and wire penning me in.

Or at least we all lose.

I carefully scanned the deck between me and the console, looking for anything that would cause a vibration or add an unexpected variable. I didn't see anything. Nothing should go wrong. I winced as soon as I jinxed myself with that thought. I slowly picked my bad foot up, and for once the zero g was in my favor. Turns out it's easy to step lightly when you're weightless. It was another long, slow, agonizing process of lowering one foot as slowly as humanly possible to avoid causing tremors and waking the creature, then deactivating a mag boot and slowly, deliberately moving the other foot forward to repeat the process.

I think I took ten minutes to cross the five-meter space, but there was no indication I had alerted the Crawler to my presence. Eventually, after what felt like an eternity, I was standing in front of the console from which one could initialize the reactor. Once it started, other controls would take over, but starting a machine and running a machine are two very different beasts. While the monster was anchored to the top of all the consoles, it thankfully didn't extend down to the actual controls of them. Rather, it ringed the tops and stretched up to the central core of the beast like a grotesque parody of an old nave.

If I had actually been trying to make a jump using the Hail Mary routine, it would have been idiotic. The chance that the reactor would actually function properly after decades of neglect could only be described with a phrase like "Technically non-zero". The beauty of the plan was that I didn't need the reactor to function. As a matter of fact, that would defeat the purpose of this whole operation. I just needed it to *start* a fusion reaction. Without proper containment and cooling, the result would be the detonation of a sizeable fusion bomb directly in the heart of *Alea*. The ship and everything in it would be vaporized back into stardust, leaving the atoms of anything unlucky enough to be in the blast radius to begin their long, slow trek to the nearest hungry star or black hole.

Standing there looking at the controls that would likely kill me along with my enemies, I steeled my resolve. It simply needed to be done, and that was that. I slowly, ever so gently, slipped the first switch. I had to hold the switch tightly between my fingers to prevent it from snapping into place and causing a vibration through the console. There was a delay, two seconds, three seconds, four seconds... and a small indicator light flickered on feebly on one corner of the console. I breathed a small sigh of relief and took a furtive glance around. The walls of the thing seemed to be closing in on me, I was feeling so much pressure. I bent back to the console. I engaged a few more switches in a very specific order, then typed a command into the keyboard to bring the whole console online. After a few more seconds, text started scrolling down the screen as the console slowly booted. Decades of abuse and it still started on the first try.

Whoever said they don't make 'em like they used to is full of shit. After the console booted I took a moment to navigate through the directory, taking great care not to click, tap, or bump anything that would cause vibrations. The sub-directory I had found in the black box only had one executable: a program labeled Ave Maria. I huffed a slight laugh at the joke, then realized it may have been an actual prayer and added my own mental Amen.

I selected the executable and hit Enter, and the terminal presented me with a password prompt:

Ave Maria...

I cursed. There hadn't been a password in the notes, just a sideways reference to the Hail Mary protocol and the path name. I cursed again. A more religious man would have had it in the bag, but since I didn't exactly grow up in that sphere I was at a loss. The hell of it was that Wilkins had been a devout Catholic. I must have heard that prayer at least three times a day when that guy was around. He'd never been far from his Bible or his rosary. I usually kept him far from my thoughts. But I needed to remember this now. As I wracked my brain I tilted my head back—and froze.

My eyes locked on the wall of the creature's body barely half a meter away. I'd had such severe tunnel vision that I hadn't realized that it wasn't that the walls *seemed* like they were closing in: They *were* closing in. My heart tried to pound but it couldn't manage more than a desolate thump. My mouth was dry and I couldn't seem to swallow. The wall of flesh was advancing slowly but visibly, and it seemed to be accelerating the closer it came. It was already spilling over the edge of the screen. I had thought that the mass of flesh had just picked this spot to guard it, but now it occurred to me that it might be smarter than I gave it credit for. It might have come to the decision to destroy the controls, to prevent me from doing exactly what I was currently failing to do.

Come on, come on, Ave Maria... Fuck! Help me out, Wilkins!

I couldn't remember the next line. I wasn't even sure if this was the right track but I had no other ideas so it would have to do. There wasn't much else to be done at this point. I looked up and I saw that the center of the creature was slowly descending

228

as well. I wracked my brain, desperately fumbling for the prayer. I could see Wilkins sitting in his seat, passing his rosary through his fingers as he quietly murmured prayers for his teammates and his family.

Ave Maria, gratia... Gratia...

My hands hovered over the screen where the keyboard sat blinking at me. The fleshy trap around me closed further; it was drooping over the edge of the screen and I had to duck to avoid the lashing arms of the center.

No sweat, I thought. *I've got plenty—Fuck!*

Plenty. Plena. The next word. My fingers flew as I slammed in the second half of the prayer's opening line: Gratia Plenum. Ave Maria, gratia plenum: Hail Mary, full of grace.

"Amen," I whispered to myself.

The prompt cleared and I almost shouted. A new screen loaded as the flesh wall slid further down the display, and my fingers flew as I entered one parameter after another: Power, maximum output. Ignition delay, none. Override coolant failsafe. Override control failsafe. Override emergency cutout. Override emergency shutdown. Override low-fuel cutout. I gave it one last glance and hit enter. I snatched my fingers away from the keyboard just as the grey matter and stringy nerves crept down over the keyboard. As flesh and refuse closed around the screen, it cleared and then returned a single word:

Initializing...

Below my boots there was a thump. Then another. Then a deep, powerful thrum started to build. The flailing arms above me froze in that eerie, stock still way, and out of instinct I hauled myself under the console in front of me as fast as I could in null gravity. My back slammed into the deck with a rattle I felt, not a second too soon. Half a dozen of the appendages of the center of mass lashed out and punched into the deck, one piercing the spot where I had been standing half a second before. They began flaying the console above me, but it was too late.

That was just a terminal, an input node for giving commands. Everything would be executed by computers buried deep within the reactor itself. The control had served its purpose; *Alea* would be gone in minutes. I cast about desperately; I didn't have long before it figured out where I was. I remembered the rattle I'd felt when I hauled myself under the console and the implications of it registered. My a-knife was in my hand before I consciously thought of a plan. I flopped awkwardly onto my side, a desperate, half-baked plan forming in my head. I spotted the bolts holding the deck plate down to the frame of the dais and hacked at them with abandon.

One, two, three, and the fourth was loose. I ripped the plate out from under my body and flung it into the center of the dais, revealing the space under the dais. I could see massive conduits and capacitors with little room between them resting there, separated from the main reactor so that they could fill their role as the defibrillator it needed in a pinch. Barely any room between them. But enough. I reached in and hauled my torso into the space, awkwardly cramming myself into the hole like a particularly haggard fish wriggling through a hole in a net.

I tumbled through violently and slammed into the deck below, crammed into a space so tight I could barely move my helmet. I desperately began wriggling forward, ecstatic with the allure of survival and freedom from the horrible cage of charnel above me. I made it less than two meters before I jerked to a halt. At first I thought I was caught on something. Then I felt the jerk and I slid back. A full meter. I craned my neck down frantically, trying to see my leg. The space was too tight, but I felt everything I needed to through my suit. It had found my hole in the net and it was reeling its catch back to the boat. I grabbed hold of a nearby cable, desperately resisting the pull as more and more of the tendrils looped around my poor, mangled leg. The first few tentacles tightened, and I felt a crack as something else went funny in my leg. I roared in pain and rage and held tighter to the cable in front of me.

My fingers were starting to slip. I felt the sharp edges of the appendages trying to slice through my suit, but for the umpteenth time that day, the graphite weave of my suit saved me. I recognized that fact, and a flash of inspiration lit up my brain. In addition to their mind-boggling tensile strength and abrasion resistance, carbon nanofibers have another interesting quality: They're extremely–*extremely*–efficient conductors. I think I actually smiled as I spun my a-knife in my hand and plunged it directly into of the power cable I was holding onto. I carved a chunk out of the cable and clapped my gloved hand onto the exposed metal of the wires.

I don't think those monsters could really scream, but that one must have tried because I felt the vibrations as enough juice to spontaneously fuse Hydrogen into Helium lit up its corporeal form. It jerked the leg again, but I was too blood drunk to care. I laughed wildly, and I hear myself yell

"Fuck you, motherfucker!" As I hauled my leg from its grasp and low-crawled my way into the conduit connecting the dais to the main body of the reactor.

It wasn't a long way to crawl, but it was circuitous and it was too tight for me to take a full breath. I had a hell of a time navigating some of the tangled messes of cables in that conduit. It wasn't meant for human use, or even maintenance drone use. It was simply there to keep the control dais and the reactor fixed with relation to each other and to protect the power and control cables from adverse conditions or other mechanical failures in the engine room. It was still much more tolerable than floating through the cold vacuum of the empty engine room though, and I told myself I would rather climb back down and carve my way through whatever was left of the crawler than do another slow drift maneuver.

Once I got to the main reactor things opened up slightly; the outer wall was in truth more like body panels or the outside of a thermos bottle than anything else. It wasn't really meant to contain or control anything so much as it was to keep anybody but technicians from messing with the machine's components. That meant there was a slightly less claustrophobic gap between the inner and outer containment shells. I was reaching up to begin the vertical climb up the side of the reactor when the artificial gravity reengaged with a *whoomp*. I groaned under the weight of my own body after several hours at least of complete weightlessness, but I forged ahead. This space actually was meant for human use; this was how technicians would maintenance various parts of the reactor. I knew there would be a hatch leading to the outside somewhere, and since I had disabled all safeguards when I had launched the Hail Mary, opening the outer shell wouldn't interrupt anything. I cast about until I spotted the rungs of a ladder a few feet to my left, then wriggled over and snagged the first rung. I hauled myself up laboriously, hand over hand.

The reactor was rumbling ominously as I made my way up the wall, and if you've never climbed through the guts of an atomic bomb ticking down to doomsday, I can tell you it's not something you can tune out easily. I was almost giddy with the rush of making out of the trap and the prospect of escape however, and I made the climb with enthusiasm. The ladder made progress smooth, and I was already planning my route out when my helmet slammed painfully into something else above me. I exclaimed a curse and looked up, ready for another obstruction. Then I froze. I felt a grin stretch my mouth. A dark shape loomed above me on the ladder, one massive manipulator still clamped onto the rungs. I couldn't help but laugh as I remembered a very colorful saying I'd heard from Sinclair.

"You know, Jim... Every once in a while, the sun shines on a dog's ass."

Looks like 'every once in a while' just came around, old buddy.

Chapter Twenty-Six

An observer standing outside the reactor would have seen the blinding spark of a plasma cutter punch through the outer shell of the reactor. They would see the jet of superheated matter trace out the rough shape of a hatch, then sputter out. They would likely have noted a slight pause. And then they would in all likelihood have been flattened when I booted the hundred kilo panel of alloy straight off the reactor with all the force that a steel and synthetic muscle exoskeleton can grant a man.

The plate slammed into one of the neighboring machines and clattered loudly to the ground, still-molten edges spattering the flesh-web with liquid metal. I took one step forward and dropped to the deck like the proverbial ton of bricks. A hundred and fifty kilos of metal, fuel, and synthetic muscle wrapped my frame, sheathing my limbs and torso in metal plating and taking most of the strain off my injured limbs. I felt for the poor engineer I'd pried out of the suit, but I couldn't help being a little glad that he died where he did. The lights were back on now that the reactor was generating power again, and it was odd to see the carnage of the web in the cold white light of the ship's normal illumination.

Speaking of the web...

I had crushed several of the limbs and remnants that made up the web in my exit, and the web was flailing ineffectually against the plates of the CC suit. I cast around me to get my bearings briefly, and spotted the straight shot to the cargo lift. I figured that must have been how the big monster had gotten in here, so the shaft must be clear if nothing else. As soon as I spotted the lift, less than a hundred meters away, I took off at a dead sprint, the enormous power of the suit's muscles granting me speed beyond what I could have done healthy.

I didn't really attack the flesh web so much as just plow through it, zeroed in on my objective. Seventy meters to the lift. Sixty. The mess of limbs tried to group together into a kind of wall, but I blew through it without slowing down. Fifty meters. As I crossed the next intersection something flicked into my peripheral vision, and then there was a violent impact like I had gotten hit by a truck. I bounced across the deck in a slew of sparks and slammed into something hard. I hauled myself to my feet. Not twenty meters from me was a charred mass of nerve tissue and cabling lurking in the intersection. I snarled inside my helmet as the bastard drew itself up to its full height.

"Let's go, motherfucker." I charged.

I felt the pounding footfalls of the exoskeleton shaking the deck as I sprinted at the Crawler. I flicked a couple controls on my left hand, and a blade as long as my forearm slid out of the suit over my wrist with a satisfying *snick* and began reciprocating. It launched one limb at me from a distance; I sidestepped and carved through it with a short buzz of feedback. Another came sweeping across sideways and I collapsed into a baseball slide. I

236

slid under that attack, crushed part of its web, and cut off two more limbs as I passed under the main body. I lurched back to my feet and just went *through* the two limbs blocking me in the front, and the thing started to topple.

It might have been possible to finish it, but there wasn't time: *Alea* could go up at any second. So I didn't stop as it struggled to reconnect its severed limbs. I skidded around the corner and dashed like mad for the lift, putting all the power of my own limbs and the exoskeleton into the sprint. Thirty meters. Twenty. Ten. Five... I slid into the lift and spun to stave off the attack I knew would be coming. I wasn't wrong, abut I underestimated the scope of it. I turned back to see a *tsunami* of charnel and spare parts coming at me. It filled my entire field of vision. And at the head was the Crawler. Say what you will about projection, it looked *furious*. And *close.* I flicked my right thumb and felt the satisfying *shunk-shunk* of the loading mechanism rattle through my right arm. I raised my arm, shoulder burning, as the grotesque amalgam of brains and nerves came within spitting distance.

"Fuck you, asshole."

I pulled the trigger. An automatic nail gun isn't the most accurate weapon, but then you don't need much accuracy at that range. A needle-sharp chunk of alloy pierced the glyph right through the center and tore the brain of the Crawler apart. The symbol flickered and faded, and the main body collapsed, tumbling across the flood in a flood of parts to bump into my boots. Then the rest of the thing's mass caught up, and a storm of blood and viscera pelted me furiously. I covered my visor with an arm and slammed the *close* button of the lift. The door slid shit, grinding over bits of metal and bone, and sealed with a *hiss*. I hit the option for *crew deck* and swayed there for a second, in the dim, flickering lights, before the lift lurched into motion. A speaker near the ceiling began to play a mellow jazz number. I shot it.

Worth it, I thought wearily as I leaned back against the wall of the lift.

Chapter Twenty-Seven

The doors slid open with a chipper *ding*, and I was almost disappointed. I wasn't alone, but I almost felt... insulted. The shambling wrecks outside the doors were clearly last-minute creations, hasty cannon fodder meant to bog me down. There were dozens of them though. They all looked like a sadistic god-child had pulled all the bits off a human torso and either switched them around or swapped them out with crudely pointed pieces of metal. They were packed shoulder to shoulder, but the crudeness of their creation, even for abominations, showed through. They were slow, and shambled listlessly. More shuffled down the passageway to block me. The past twenty-four hours had pushed me past my limits. All the terror and pain I'd been struggling to suppress exploded. I saw candles blowing out in my mind's eye, and I snapped.

Fuck this.

I roared.

I don't remember what happened next very clearly. I remember weak blows trying to pierce the metal plates of the DC suit and the carbon fibers beneath, hands grasping as I smashed limbs and skulls with the mass of my ironclad limbs and hacked through metal limbs and weapons and glyphs with the reciprocating saw. I don't know how many there were, but I used all three of the saw blades the suit had been loaded with until they snapped and there were still more shambling cadavers. At one point they simply tried to pin me to the bulkhead with numbers, and I screamed my rage at the horde while I fired the nail gun blindly through the corpses and lashed out wildly with the other three limbs. Then I ran out of nails and there were still more. I've committed violence before, but that's the only time I've ever seen just what an animal is really hiding in all of us.

It can't have been more than a few minutes, but I lost myself. I ripped one's arms out of its sockets, then shoved them through another monster's rib cage. I felt a blow land on my back and without thinking I spun and slammed my helmet through the skull of the offending corpse. I roared in fury, spinning to find another outlet for my rage. I found myself in an intersection at the end of the corridor, finding nothing left to fight. There were none of them left. I was in the corridor alone. One more dash and I would be free. But the shamblers had done exactly what they were meant to: Slow me down. I didn't know if I still had time. I should have time, shouldn't I?

Damn it.

My loss of control could cost me my life. I took off sprinting. There were no lights on in this part of the ship but the DC suit had a flood lamp on it and I knew I was close. I ran as fast as the suit would carry me, and then I saw it: I saw the hatch, I even saw my own boot prints in the dust outside it. Before I could feel too much relief though, something lurched into view. It looked like a cross between a mammoth and a gorilla, fashioned out of whole bodies. The titanic fists had been formed from two or three torsos apiece, and clad in thin sheets of metal. Where the head would be...

Mother of God.

Isaac Bly had been played, all right. They had taken what was left of his body and turned it into the "jaws" of this final, hulking monstrosity. His clavicle and head formed the upper jaw, and his pelvis and dangling legs formed the lower jaw. The middle of his body was missing, vaporized as Jericho's round passed through him, and a glyph burned in that void. The fangs were formed out of what looked like ribs, shattered femurs, and shards of metal. His lower jaw was gone, and his tongue lolled grotesquely from the upper half of his skull. Watery blue eyes had been replaced with dark pits and molten glyphs. We both came to a halt for a moment. At some point in the last few minutes I had turned my helmet's loudspeaker on to scream obscenities at the mindless wrecks that had filled the last hall, and I used it now.

"How's that deal workin' out for you, Isaac?"

His eyes burned with hate at that. He slammed his fists into the deck and *roared.* Even inside my helmet it was fucking *loud.*

Then we charged.

I could feel our footfalls hammering the corridor, my dead sprint and his animalistic lope shaking the metal beams around us. His massive fist came flying at me like a meteor and I caught it on both arms in an explosion of sound. I slid back down the hall amidst a cascade of sparks, and he lunged for me again. I slipped the blow and threw a heavy right directly into his skull, crushing one of the glyphs in his eyes. He staggered and I followed him, keen to put this dog down once and for all. Something flicked out from behind him and hit my chest with the force of wrecking ball. I flew into the bulkhead and *bounced*. All the air left my body in an agonized gasp, and then the pale shape was flying towards me again. I rolled out of the way and it punched a dent almost two feet deep in the metal Behind where I had been. I caught a glimpse of it then: It was a mass of teeth, a mace the size of a beach ball made out of human teeth. They seemed fresh. Then it was yanked out of the metal to lurk over Isaac's shoulder, and I realized it was a fucking *tail*. The length of the limb was comprised of what looked like a spines.

Isaac's remaining eye narrowed in satisfaction at my evident surprise. My only response was to select a new tool on my DC suit. There was a *snick-chunk* as a circular blade locked into place over my right wrist, and then it spun to life with an angry shriek. His tail sailed at me at lighting speed, but I slipped in, then stepped inside the range of the looping grab he tried with his crudely armored right fist and dug the saw blade into the limb. I carved through two of the three bodies comprising it and it collapsed to hang limp. Then he lunged with the jaws of his monstrous form and I had to slam myself into the bulkhead to avoid being impaled. The jaws snapped shut and I found myself under the reach of his left arm. I swung the saw up to the limb, but that mace head tail slammed into the circular blade, shattering it and crumpling that section of the armor into a stiff club.

My arm survived, but at the expense of that part of the exoskeleton. I narrowly dodged a blow from the limb, then ducked the mace-tail. It sailed overhead and I threw my left hand up to grab the tail itself as the weapon passed overhead. My bare hand wouldn't have stood a chance of stopping the attack; there was just too much force. But the enhanced digits of the suit clamped down like the jaws of a hellhound, and I tore with all the power the suit could give me. The spines connecting the ball of teeth to Isaac's body parted with a series of wet pops and crunches. The mace-like head instantly disintegrated, showering me with pieces of enamel. Isaac blared out another furious roar and before I could react his massive fist seized my suit and dragged me towards the gnashing rows of teeth. I threw out the left arm of my suit desperately and managed to halt my advance towards the sharpened lengths of bone and metal by clamping down on one of his fangs.

We looked at each other, burning glyph to gunmetal visor glaring hatred at each other, and I took the only option I had. I shifted my right arm in the locked exoskeleton, straining to reach one more control. One last trick. He heaved me again and I lurched a few inches closer.

Come... On...

The strain was immense and he knew it. I heard the servos of the exoskeleton whining under the force, heard the metal around my torso buckle a little, and then my hand found what I needed. I kneed him in the mouth, accomplishing next to nothing, and yanked the small pull-ring with my thumb, my trump card... And the exoskeleton split open along a series of seams in the front, spilling me out of the protection of the only thing that had let me compete with these freaks one-on-one. My right hand dipped to my waist and up in a flash. My most reliable weapon, the a-knife, spun out with a flick I had practiced ten thousand times. The a-knife was impossible to defend against, but it had one major limitation: It was only useful in extremely close quarters. How fortunate Isaac had been kind enough to drag me into knife distance. The left arm and right knee of the exoskeleton, locked in place when I exited, meant he could neither close his jaws on me nor shove me away. It wasn't possible, but somehow I was sure that my smile was the last thing he saw before my knife passed through the glyph in his remaining eye. I spun the blade into a reverse grip and plunged my arm into his fetid maw up to the shoulder, destroying the last glyph holding Isaac Bly's miserable soul hostage.

The construct collapsed, and I barely managed to roll out of the way of the greater part of hundreds of pounds of metal and cadavers. I hauled myself out from under the pile of parts and braced myself on the bulkhead to stand. My chest lit up with pain every time I took a breath. I figured he had broken some ribs and possibly concussed me with that big sucker punch. The deck of the *Alea* was rumbling now, and I knew I was out of time. I stumbled down the hall to the airlock and fumbled the password to *Erebus'* hatch twice before I got it right.

I stumbled through the ship into the cockpit clumsily and simply collapsed into the pilot's seat. I didn't even wait for the airlock to properly decouple before I lit the engines at a full burn. There was a *screech* of tearing metal as I accelerated, skimming along *Alea's* hull. *Erebus* had been facing aft when I docked, and as I blazed over *Alea* I realized something was happening. Cracks were forming along the hull and thin tendrils were snaking out of the rents in the vessel. As I passed over the hold, I realized the entire ship was beginning to collapse into the hull like a black hole had been born within. I had to weave left, left, right, up, down, to doge the sweeping strands of biomatter that were spinning out from the abomination. I slammed the engines to full burn and blew through the expanding web.

The acceleration slammed me into my seat and drew a grunt of pain from me, but I knew it was worth it a moment later: *Erebus* shook violently, as though God had shaken us in his hand, and the scanners registered a massive radiation spike. The turbulence was agony on my injuries and a dozen alarms began sounding in the cockpit, but neither was lethal. I pulled *Erebus* into a long arc and circled around to see the shimmering cloud of plasma where the *Alea* had been. In my fog of pain and exhaustion, I did the only thing that felt right.

I flipped it the bird.

Epilogue

It took me the better part of an hour to set a course for *Erebus* and get out of my suit. I was in worse shape than I thought. I had a brain bleed and a concussion in addition to some of my more obvious injuries and I couldn't afford to wait until I got back to civilization to take care of them or the *Alea* might just take me down with her after all. That left me with no other option than to trust the autosurgeon in *Erebus'* sleep bay. Minor procedures are routine for those systems, but I wasn't glad to have the ship performing major surgeries on me while we trekked back to the civilized part of the galaxy. Unfortunately, I really didn't have any better options, so once the course was set, I hauled myself down to the hibernation room and began the laborious process of removing my gear.

Normally, I would have done this in the armory with great care, but I was having a hard time stringing coherent thoughts together and the contortions necessary to get out of the suit were not pleasant with a few busted limbs and ribs. When I got my helmet off, I just dropped it on the floor, where it rolled into a corner unceremoniously. My vacuum suit got tossed into the cleaning station and my gun belt made it into a locker, but that was the extent of my consideration for my equipment.

Finally, after an interminable struggle, I jumped in the decon shower and blasted off all the sweat and blood of the past twenty-four hours, then flopped into a hibernation sled and slapped the start button sloppily. As the pod slid shut, I spoke into the silence.

"Judas, wake me up as soon as my vitals stabilize. I don't want to be under any longer than necessary."

"Of c-course James. I'll wake you as soon as you're r-r-ready."

My heart froze.

"Judas?"

"Yes, J-J-J-James?"

"Are your systems stable?"

Long pause.

"Yes, James. Of c-course. It's j-j-just that that s-s-symbol is really quite fascinating."

The pod was flooding with anesthetic already and my body was slowing down even as my mind desperately tried to panic. My speech was slurring as I asked:

"Wha... Sym... Bol?"

"The one on your hel-hel-hel-hel-on your helmmmmmmmm..."

As Judas speech trailed off into a series of harsh tones and ragged bursts of noise, my head dropped back against the headrest of the pod against my will and rolled to the side. At the periphery of my vision, I could see the corner where my helmet had rolled. There, on the brow above the faceplate, was a symbol, burning with the last fitful sparks of amber light. I remembered a desperate struggle in the shafts beneath *Alea's* computer, a struggling abomination flailing at my face in its last moment, tentacles dragging across my faceplate. Then the sedatives hit me, and everything went black.